# Dire Water

**Story By**

Thomas Knapp

**Based on MegaTokyo: Endgames By**

Fred Gallagher

**Editor**

Ray Kremer

# Chapter One: The Orphanage in the Woods

*She was tired and cold. Why had mommy woken her up so early?*

*"Hush, little one. Please don't cry. We have to leave."*

*Leave? Why? What was going on?*

*Her mother made sure that the coat was closed tight, with the hood covering almost all of her face. Her tail had been tucked painfully into the back of the coat, which was the source of her discomfort.*

*"I know it hurts, but you can't let anyone see until we're far away from the palace. Don't talk, don't cry, just let me carry you."*

*She still didn't know what was going on. Why did they have to leave?*

*"V? Where V?" She finally asked.*

*"She isn't coming. We're going to where* ***I*** *came from," Her mother said. "We probably won't ever come back."*

***That*** *got her to cry.*

*"Baby... please... stop!" Her mother begged frantically. "You mustn't make noise! They'll kill us!"*

*She abruptly stopped, and blinked. Kill? Who? What?*

*"Please... don't ask questions. Just be quiet, keep your ears and tail hidden, and we'll be all right."*

*She frowned, but stayed silent. Her mother wasn't one to lie. If there was danger, she needed to listen.*

*"There's going to be a changing of the guard soon, and that's when we need to make our escape."*

*She wasn't really paying attention to her mother at that point. She was still coming to grips with leaving, and never coming back. She'd never see Viola again, or Macy, or Darcy, or... anyone. She didn't know anything about where her mother was from other than it being far to the south. She knew Viola used to go there with her family, but that was it.*

*"Sunay!"*

~ ~ ~ ~ ~

"Sunay!"

Her ears twitched, but otherwise she didn't stir. If it was *that* important, Matron Miriam would yell louder.

"***SUNAY!***"

Like that.

Sunay stirred slowly, uncurling from the fetal position before pushing herself up to hands and knees. With a wide yawn, she pushed her arms forward to stretch them out, then extended her legs to do the same. From there, she arched her back, and shook the sleep out of her bones starting from her shoulders and working down to the tip of her tail.

"***SUNAY!***"

"Coders! I'm comin'!" Sunay roared in annoyance. Matron Miriam was always such a worrywart.

Sunay dropped to all fours, finding that while it didn't really improve her speed, she felt more stable navigating the rough forest floor, allowing her to move faster more confidently. Skipping over exposed roots and shuffling through tall grass, she burst from the foliage into the clearing where Miriam's Orphanage resided.

If you didn't know it was there, chances of your finding it were slim. As far as Sunay knew, the nearest town in any direction was through five miles of forest. The only road was a road in name only, shrouded by low branches and ferns, barely enough to let Miriam's single horse drawn cart through. Her orphanage was well hidden, and kept very quiet by anyone who might have known of its existence.

There was good reason for that. Miriam's Orphanage was a home for lost, abandoned, or orphaned chimeras.

Chimeras had a rough life in the Republican Provinces of Avalon, and they kept to themselves for good reason. Nobles and royalty of the previous era had curses cast upon their significant others to make sure they didn't sow their wild oats. Chimeras were the result of such cursed nobles' lack of faithfulness to their spouses. As a result, such children were easy to identify and scorn.

On the other side, in the new age run by the Parliament, chimeras were still considered members of the noble families that had been overthrown, and as such were often executed upon capture. Rejected by their noble parents, and scorned by their commoner kin, there were very few places of refuge for the hundreds, if not thousands, of poor literal bastards.

Which explained Matron Miriam's constant worry whenever Sunay turned up missing. "How many times have I told you not to go sleeping in the woods?" she demanded with exasperation.

Sunay dismissed the concern, like she always did. "And how many times has nuthin' happened to me?"

"There are hunting parties from the north this season," Miriam scolded. "They are starting *fox* hunts."

Sunay rolled her eyes. "Ya been sayin' that fer the last five summers."

"And I really wish you would speak properly."

"Feh."

"Coders as my witness, if only you were so influenced by one appearance in the classroom. You run off against my direct orders, see a pirate ship from the beach *one* time, and it ruins all the education I tried to push into your skull."

Sunay grit her teeth and frowned. So what if that was true? So what if she wanted to do more than hide in some crumbling old building in the middle of nowhere, and a life on the lawless seas was the only way she could do that. So maybe she *did* admire that way of life. What about it?

The matron surrendered. She turned about, and said, "Hurry up inside at the very least. Supper is about to start, and the rest of the kids won't start eating without you."

Sunay highly doubted that, but knew it was better to stop arguing and go inside.

The orphanage was in fact a converted church... though not the grand cathedrals devoted to worship of the Coders, the supposed deities that fashioned the world. This was most likely a church for more unconventional services, though it wasn't something Matron Miriam encouraged her many charges to think about. It was a construct of wood, thatch, and no doubt several prayers that it wouldn't all come crashing down in the middle of the night.

The interior at least looked a lot better than the outside. With ten rooms all neatly divided, it provided enough space for the denizens to eat and sleep, if little much else. But it was a dry roof over their heads, which was more than a chimera could expect on her own.

"Matron! The roof's got a hole again!"

Well... a *mostly* dry roof.

Megan was probably the sweetest, innocent, most loving twelve-year-old girl and would have no doubt been snatched up by the first loving couple that saw her, if it wasn't for her big drooping black dog ears with white spots and six thin white whiskers that sprouted from her cheeks.

Sunay was fairly lucky with her curse, as her ears and tail

could be *somewhat* hidden if they absolutely had to be. It really hurt her tail to tuck that bushy thing in her drawers, but she *could*. Most chimeras didn't even have that luxury. They had whiskers, discolored spots, or patches of fur that were extremely difficult to hide.

Matron Miriam didn't even need to ask. Sunay knew her role in the orphanage. "I'll patch it up after dinner."

"Thank you, Sunay," the matron replied tenderly. "I suspect rain is coming tomorrow. But for now, Kaeli no doubt has dinner ready."

Kaeli was a bear, in both the figurative and literal sense. A large, imposing woman with a thin brown coat of hair, and looked just like her animal half when she was on her hands and knees if you weren't looking particularly closely. Her keen sense of smell made her quite a capable cook despite the less-than-excellent ingredients the orphanage had at their disposal.

The fare was simple, but tasty and plentiful enough to fill bellies, which was what mattered at the end of the day. This was especially important for Sunay, who really didn't want to pass out from hunger while climbing around on the church's roof.

There was a time when Sunay grumbled about the work she had to do, but as one of the oldest remaining orphans, she had a responsibility to the wee ones, and was one of the few suited to do the heavier labor and maintenance on the aging building. Sunay still didn't know how Matron Miriam handled such duties by herself without the spryness a curse like Sunay's could provide.

Sunay first hefted a panel of thin flexible pinewood up the ladder and onto the roof in question. It was fortunate that the southern coast of Avalon was so warm, because the wood she had to use wouldn't have kept out even a mild chill, much less the bitter cold Sunay could vaguely remember from her early years in Caravel, the capital of the Republic.

She climbed back down the ladder two more times to get a bucket of tar and a small bale of straw that would form the patch she needed. With all the necessary supplies, Sunay finally got to assessing the damage from above. It wasn't too bad, she had known that from looking it over from below earlier, but big enough to drench a good section of the little one's sleeping space if left in disrepair.

The first thing she had to do was clear enough thatch from the damaged section so she could lay the pine panel over the hole. This was probably the hardest part of the project, as dried tar did not like to release whatever it had in its clutches, and thatch broke too easily for her to just pry it loose. It required an application of a hammer and chisel to break up the tar and give her the space she needed.

Sunay didn't particularly care exactly where she threw the hunks of debris as long as they were no longer on the roof. The rest of the orphans knew she was working, so if they got brained, it was their own damned fault. She could pick up those scraps later after she was done.

She stuck a line of five nails between her lips, and swiftly began hammering the panel to the others, replacing the nails as needed. Normally, she would try and find supports to nail the wood into, but there wasn't any sturdier wood around the hole, so she had to improvise and hope it held through the coming fall storm season. It should; the fall storms were never as bad as the spring typhoons that could decimate the coast even hundreds of miles inland. Hopefully they would have the money and resources to replace that entire section of the roof before next spring.

With the panel nailed in, she took a deep breath in preparation for the second hardest part of the job, churning the tar in the bucket with a long piece of wood so that it was pliable enough to spread on the panel. It didn't help at all that the tar had started cooling the moment it was taken off the heat, making the process even more difficult than helping Kaeli mix molasses that had managed to damn near freeze last winter.

Sunay was sweating heavily by the time she deemed the tar able to be spread, her chest heaving with each tired breath as she slapped globs of the sticky black substance on the pine panel, and grunting as she forced the tar to spread into a thick layer across the wood.

At least the last part of the process was fairly easy, at least relatively, spreading the straw over the tar to finish the cover that would keep the elements at bay. What straw didn't stick would get blown off by wind, so she didn't waste too much time with the clean-up. It was getting late, and she wanted to get off that damned roof.

The trip down was a lot easier when she only had to bring down the bucket, and dropped that off outside the kitchen door for Kaeli to deal with while Sunay went back to collect the bigger pieces of old tar she had discarded. Those she disposed of in the trash pit at the edge of the clearing to be burned when it got full enough. Sunay really didn't want to be there for that. Burning tar smelled horrible to begin with, and it wasn't going to be any sweeter with all the other garbage as well.

Kaeli wasn't entirely happy that Sunay left the tar outside the door rather than clean it out, at least until she saw Sunay finally slump back into the building. "Oh! And here I was about to yell at you!" the bear-woman said. "You're straight tuckered out, aren't ya?"

"I'll... scrub the bucket t'morrow," Sunay said. "Promise ya."

Kaeli enveloped Sunay in a big hug, and patted the foxgirl on the top of the head. "Nah, don't you worry about it. That hole probably needed a whole lot of work. Let ol' Kaeli take care of it. You get some rest."

Sunay would normally argue, but right now she didn't have the energy to willingly take on work that someone else was offering to do. "Thanks, Kae. I'll make it up t'ya."

"Ah, you know we don't keep score here."

Sunay knew that was true enough. Everyone helped however they could. There wasn't room for arguments about who did more work and when; Matron Miriam made sure of that. "'Ave a good night, Kae," Sunay said with as pleasant of a smile as she could manage, before leaving the kitchen and into the main hall.

The children had shuffled off to their various rooms in anticipation of sleep, the matron's curfew of in bed by nightfall strictly enforced. You didn't actually have to be *asleep,* and children rarely were, but you had to at least be in your room so you could be counted. Miriam was serious about knowing where her charges were at night.

In fact, Sunay was a bit surprised to see that the matron wasn't already on her roll call. Miriam's door was still closed, only the faint glow of candlelight an indication that she was inside. The foxgirl pressed her ear against the door, her eyebrows furrowing in concentration, catching the sounds of sobbing from the other side, the matron clearly trying to keep the noise as quiet as possible.

"Matron, ma'am?" Sunay said with concern, also trying to keep her voice down so that only the matron could hear. "Ya okay in there?"

"Oh!" Miriam exclaimed before regaining her composure. "Sunay! Come in, child."

Something was very wrong, which Sunay confirmed when she opened the door to see the matron slumped forward in her chair, head resting on her arms on the desk in front of her, flanked by two rose scented candles. Those were sacramental candles.

The ones Coders' Acolytes burned in remembrance.

Sunay's ears drooped. "Oh Coders... who was it?"

"Raquel and John," Miriam said. "I got the letter from the

Line masters this morning. The convoy heading to Aramathea was found."

The "Line" referred to a small underground movement of sorts that tried to help chimeras, along with political opponents to the Parliament and general criminals, try to escape Avalon either into the Free Provinces or the southern empire of Aramathea.

Raquel and John were two of the "first generation" of orphans after the revolution, and had tried to get out of the country and build a life of their own on the Gold Coast. Sunay suspected that Raquel was pregnant, and probably the driving force that prompted them to leave the orphanage. Miriam had tried to convince them to stay... and the matron's instincts had apparently been right.

"I trust you don't need any details," Miriam said with blatant melancholy.

Sunay knelt down to give the matron a comforting hug. "Nah, I don't." How Avalon dealt with chimeras was common knowledge: you were tied to a post and burned alive. Members of the Church of the Coders believed that destroyed the animal spirit possessing the chimera. It was ridiculous of course; even *if* the chimera was "natural" in that fashion, spirits weren't destroyed by physical fire. And even if that *did* work, the only thing it did for the cursed noble chimeras was give them one of the most agonizing deaths possible.

It was during that closeness to the matron that Sunay smelled the telltale tingle of alcohol, and became aware of the half empty bottle of wine on Miriam's desk. "Are... are you okay, ma'am?" Sunay asked, nervously pointing to the bottle.

Miriam answered by standing up, grabbing a second glass, and pouring out another round, offering the second glass to Sunay. "Pull up a chair, child. You probably need it as much as I."

Sunay complied, taking and turning one of the chairs on the east wall of the room. She was no stranger to wine, something Miriam began allowing the foxgirl to have when she turned fifteen last winter, but it was still something that wasn't readily offered except on rare occasions. Sunay took a sip so that the tart liquid could instill some of its courage, and asked, "Is something else wrong, ma'am?"

Matron Miriam normally carried herself with such strength, and it was disconcerting to see her look so defeated. Miriam slumped backward in her chair, and shook her head. "Just... remembering all those who have been lost over the years. Each one hurts. And the pain builds on itself each time I get such terrible news. Jacob... Peter... Paul... Mary... poor Mary. Poor, poor, Mary."

Mary had been a victim of the bad part of the Line three years ago. As an underground movement, there was very little in the way of quality control, and you could just as easily wind up a victim of other less savory individuals using the Line, or even the Line handlers themselves. Mary... had been found by other Line handlers, tied up, raped, and eventually killed after whoever was responsible had tired of her.

"You're not going to leave, are you, Sunay?" Miriam asked fearfully.

Sunay smiled after another swallow of wine. "No plans to, ma'am. Where woulda I go even if'n I wanted?"

Miriam cringed at Sunay's butchery of the spoken word, but replied, "Even if I don't like how you said it, I'm happy to hear it nonetheless."

The pair shared a subdued chuckle before the mood quickly turned back to somber. "I still remember exactly when you and your mother arrived. I'm so very sorry there was nothing I could do for her." Miriam didn't even try to hide her regret.

Sunay also was regretful, but for a different reason. "I don't even 'member too much 'bout it, prob'ly why I'm not too upset."

"You were so young. Just past your second birthday when you and your mother arrived in the spring," Miriam said. This was a story Sunay had heard before, but she didn't want to interrupt the matron who clearly needed this vent. "She was so sick to begin with, afflicted with the 'Noble's Disease.' The bastard who got her sick... I hope he burns in the white hot coals of the Forsaken Pit. The Void would be too good for him."

"All the hurt and pain chimeras suffer," Miriam snarled bitterly, her face twisting with simmering rage. "For what reason? Because they were the result of base and carnal noblemen abusing servants? The people hurt *most* by the old ways, and the Republic makes things *worse*. How is that the behavior of fair and just gods?"

"It ain't, but it don' matter, ma'am," Sunay said. "You been all the just and fair that I've ever seen."

"But I wish I could do so much more. You and yours should have more than a broken down church hidden in a forest. You should be able to live freely where you wish. You should be able to marry and have children without lying with murderers and bandits on an illegal trade route. I... why can't I give you these things?"

"Because yer one woman who's doing more than she can already. Nonna us blame ya at all."

Miriam sobbed, her chest heaving with tears she was trying to hold back. "Sunay, child, can you do the roll call tonight? I don't want the kids to see me like this."

"Of course, ma'am. You... ya just be okay," Sunay tripped over her tongue as she repeated, "Okay?"

Miriam sighed in resignation, "I don't have the energy to correct your horrible grammar tonight."

Some things never changed.

With a comforting pat on Miriam's shoulder, Sunay left to do the nightly roll call. It was so important to make sure everyone was present. Having to do a late night search for a missing child was potentially dangerous, as visible torches and lanterns in the woods could draw unwanted attention, even as secluded as the old church was.

The first room contained the littlest ones. Harold, Artemis, Clive, and Andrew. Harold, Artemis, and Clive were six, Andrew seven. All of them had been abandoned to the orphanage, most likely by noblemen or women who couldn't hide their status with growing children who would get increasingly more difficult to hide.

Chimeras didn't get much younger than that at this point, the nobles cursed in such a fashion having finally found ways out of Avalon, either to the north in Tortuga, to the east towards the Free Provinces, or southeast towards Aramathea. If chimera children hadn't fled the country or found refuge at this point... they likely weren't going to.

Like the case of Liam. Liam had literal scales, snake eyes, and a forked tongue. Matron Miriam had heard about the boy in a nearby town and discovered upon arrival that he had been beaten then burned to death days before she got there. A four year old kid.

Liam didn't last long upon being discovered.

Few chimeras did.

The next five rooms held the "second wave" of chimeras, like Megan, and they represented the majority that remained within the orphanage. They were all around the ages of ten to twelve, and were the result of nobles trying to hide shortly after the revolution, often maliciously abandoning the cursed children born of their philandering ways rather than risk being outed as a noble. During the period when *these* children were found, the animosity wasn't quite as high in the southern provinces as it was in the north. Those who found themselves in the right hands were spared, and eventually found their way to the orphanage.

The last two rooms were where the "first wave" of orphans

stayed, like Sunay and Kaeli, as well as the few adults who remained as volunteers. These were chimeras and normal humans who had lived through the time of the revolution thirteen years ago. Some of them, like Kaeli, remembered life under the monarchy, and how they'd traded one life of destitution for another.

These "old folks" just never got a break.

All were accounted for, which was a minor mercy, as that was something that rarely happened whenever there were fifty-seven people to keep track of. Sunay reported the good news to Matron Miriam, finished the glass of wine Miriam had poured for her, then retreated to her room.

She shared said room with three other people, other "first wave" orphans, their sleeping bags arranged along the perimeter of the small space so that there was *some* room to move about in the middle. Kyle was already asleep, no doubt still recovering from the chill he had managed to acquire two days ago. She stepped around him, careful not to wake him, and smiled in greeting to Blake and Penelope who had been talking to each other, quietly, for that same reason.

Sunay's sleeping space was tucked into the furthest corner, and unlike the others she didn't have a sleeping bag, as she found them horribly uncomfortable. Instead, she had a pile of straw that served suitably enough for rest, as it allowed her to curl up into a ball with her tail in front of her face to block out the remaining light.

*"You're not going to leave, are you, Sunay?"*

Matron Miriam's question rung in her head as she closed her eyes. It was such a terrible question to ask. Of *course* she wanted to leave. *Everyone* in the orphanage did, and it made them feel terrible to even think about it, because it wasn't the matron's fault.

But there was a huge world out there, even if it was openly hostile. Sunay *wanted* to experience more than this small island in the storm. She wanted to feel the sea air. She wanted to be free. She wanted to live without fear. She wanted to *see* the places she had heard about in Matron Miriam's tutoring: Aramathea, Reaht, the Daynelands, the tropical islands, the Forever Seas...

At least her dreams could go there, and Sunay soon followed thanks to the fatigue of a hard day's work.

## Chapter Two: A Noble Visitor

Sunay had a system. Matron Miriam would ask her to go out in the forest to forage for mushrooms. Sunay would pretend it took her hours to find enough fungi to supplement Kaeli's vegetable stock, when in truth it took the foxgirl maybe an hour at most. She could then spend the rest of the time prowling, hunting, and napping in peace and quiet rather than surrounded by a small army of children.

A bed of straw was decent enough, but it simply didn't compare to the slightly moist earth underneath the forest canopy. Compared to the bustling church, the sounds of the forest were practically silence. The chirping birds, the hoof fall of deer, the grating howl of a foxhound...

Wait a minute.

Uh oh.

Sunay thanked the Coders for her animal reflexes as she quickly sprung out of her ball as the lean, short-haired body of a gray Avalon Foxhound burst from the foliage with another teeth-grating wail and made a swift change of direction to match Sunay's attempt to dodge its charge.

The fox proved slightly faster than the hound, at least for the first exchange, as the dog's jaws snapped angrily at empty air.

"Yah! Git outta here, mutt!" Sunay screamed, hoping that the sound of a human voice would confuse the beast that smelled fox.

It did, as the foxhound stopped dead in its tracks as it spun about for a second charge, dropping onto its hind quarters and tilted its head trying to process the conflicting information coming from its nose and ears. Sunay tried to use that indecision to make her escape when she heard another human voice approaching quickly.

"Nelly! Come here, girl! Stupid dog... we're *not* hunting foxes today. I just want a nice walk in the woods, is that *really* too much to ask? *Nelly!* Come here *now!*"

That caused Sunay to jump, literally up the nearest tree, and that sudden movement caused the hound to decide that she was more fox than human, and started barking angrily while clawing at the bark.

Sunay hissed, "Go 'way, ya damned mutt! Leave me alone!" as the dog's presumed owner emerged into view, struggling with the foliage that his hound had handled so easily.

He didn't exactly have the look of a fox hunter. He was a

slight fellow, dressed for comfort in thin brown pants and a frilled shirt covered by a cotton vest, the ensemble littered with barbed balls from the prickly ferns that grew rampant in the forest.

"Nelly!" he bellowed to the dog that continued to ignore him. "Idiot dog... why my mother insisted on making me drag you out here..."

The man grabbed the dog by the collar, and tried to pull the foxhound away. It almost worked, until the dog lunged out of its presumed master's grasp and started scratching and howling at Sunay again.

"Coders curse you, dog, you're not going to find a fox up th..."

At that point, the boy had looked up, and his eyes met Sunay's despite her efforts to hide herself in the branches.

His voice fell, now awestruck. "Okay, I stand corrected."

He was a handsome fellow, Sunay had to admit. His hair was a sandy brown, with bright blue eyes, lightly bronzed skin from the southern sun, and smooth features that had yet to suffer the wear of time.

Sunay flattened her ears and prayed to the Coders that he hadn't seen her tail. He most likely hadn't, because he wasn't cursing her to the fiery pits and trying to find a torch. "Go away!" she shouted angrily. "Take your mutt and leave me alone!"

"Oh, my dear lady, I am *so* very sorry!" he said with earnest apology, again trying to rein in the dog. "I don't know what has come over her. Are you alright?"

"I'm fine! Just go 'way!" Sunay was panicking, and she knew it. Matron Miriam would be furious at her if she found out about this.

The boy tried to pull on his dog again, this time losing his grip on the pull, falling backward and landing square on his rump on top of Sunay's discarded satchel of mushrooms. He instantly knew something was wrong due to the softness of the landing, and identified why upon standing up. "Oh no! I am so very sorry, my dear lady! Were these yours?"

"It's fine! Just leave!" Sunay shouted, her voice approaching frantic.

The boy shook his head, terrified by the thought. "I couldn't possibly, my lady! My dog and I ruined your gathering, and I would be punished so very harshly if I didn't make amends. It's the gentleman's way!"

"I don't need yer 'elp! Go!"

The boy circled the tree, his eyes narrowing in curiosity.

Sunay shifted among the branches to counter, trying as hard as she could to keep as much obstruction between them as possible.

"It's hard to tell, but had I known the orphanage had such pretty girls, I would have defied my father's order and visited in person."

Sunay jolted, and she asked nervously, "Ya... know 'bout the orphanage?"

"My father is the de facto mayor of Navarre. Where do you think your matron keeps getting her supplies?"

Sunay let her ears raise slightly, if for no reason that it wasn't entirely comfortable to lay them flat for too long. She pushed aside the branches to offer the boy a better look, and said, "You know... about us?"

The boy smiled warmly. "Of course, my lady. My grandfather was the lord of this land before the Revolution, and my father kept some authority and our family lands by siding with the rebels." he said before his voice shifted, "I'd wager that there's at least two among your number that could call me brother. It's a mutual protection, I'm sure."

"Pretty bastard move to 'ide your children in our dump of an orphanage," Sunay grumbled, deciding she didn't like this boy very much.

"I agree."

That reply took Sunay off guard. "What? You'd want 'im to claim 'is little bastards? You wouldn' be worried that they'd, I dunno..."

"I'm the youngest of my father's legitimate brats. I don't have much of an inheritance to steal. What I did have was two good friends who probably never knew who their father really was and who I have been forbidden to see since I was nine, when they were shipped off to your orphanage."

The boy tried again to harness his dog, and this time it was successful enough for him to reattach the lead to the dog's collar. "I am truly very sorry about Nelly. My mother insists I don't leave the manor without *some* sort of escort. Please do come down, Nelly is all howl and nothing else, I promise."

Getting down from a tree was always harder than going up, and it wasn't an easier process when the boy was distracting her.

"You have a very lovely tail."

Sunay blushed and growled, "You better not be talkin' 'bout mah butt."

"I wouldn't dare be so uncouth, my lady."

Confident she was finally close enough to the ground to let herself drop the rest of the way, she fell, landing with a crouch onto the forest floor. As she straightened, she said, “Coders, if we're gonna keep talkin', might as well use our names. I'm Sunay.”

“Laron,” the boy replied, offering his hand in greeting. When Sunay took the shake, he instead turned hers palm down to drop a kiss on the back of her hand.

“Oh please stop, will ya?” she said with a roll of her eyes, even as she fought back the blush already on her freckled cheeks. She found a suitable alternate focus of her attention, taking her satchel from Laron and confirming that the mushrooms inside were indeed mushed beyond salvage. With a sigh, she dumped out the satchel's contents and said, “Well, I guess it's back ta work for me.”

Laron pleaded, “Let me help you, Sunay. It was my dumb dog's fault, and I would feel terrible leaving you to have to start over all your work on your own.”

On one hand, it didn't take her very long at all to gather mushrooms. On the other, it wouldn't be a bad thing if it took even less. On the other, other hand, Laron looked like he had exactly zero experience identifying edible mushrooms. On the other, other, other hand, Sunay suspected Laron wasn't going to take no for an answer.

She bent down at the knees to pick up the most intact specimen that had been in her bag. “I'm lookin' for mushrooms like this. Think you can handle that?”

Laron nodded vigorously. “Provided Nelly doesn't try to eat them. Come on girl, let's see if your nose is good for more than foxes.”

They parted for their search, but kept in speaking distance so as to easily find each other. “It's such a shame that chimeras are so hated now,” Laron said in conversation. “Both of my siblings were so sweet, even though they were never allowed outside.”

“What were their names?” Sunay asked. “I probably know them.”

“The first one to leave was Anders. I was only five at the time. The younger one was about my age, maybe a little older. She was Raquel. If I didn't think your matron would tell on me, I would try to find your orphanage.”

Sunay's heart sank like a brick in their stomach. “I dunno about Anders. He left the orphanage 'bout five years ago; we haven't heard any news about 'im over the Line, so we can only assume that's good. Raquel... we got word a few days ago that she 'ad been caught by Republic forces tryin' ta get across the border.”

She didn't want to say anything else, and she didn't need to. She could see him between two trees stop in his tracks, and his sobs heaving his chest.

Sunay had seen too many people crying recently. She navigated the distance, ignored Nelly's warning growl, and wrapped her arms around Laron's shoulders. She didn't know what else to say. When she'd learned about it, she had wanted to cry too. "Ya both were real close, eh?"

"Raquel and I were about the same age. She probably would have been sent to the orphanage sooner, but my mother didn't want to abandon her." He laughed once at the memory. "Funny that, isn't it? My mother didn't want to abandon my father's illegitimate child."

"Kinda odd fer the woman who woulda 'ad 'er 'usband cursed," Sunay replied.

Laron shook his head. "She wasn't the one responsible for the curse. She honestly wasn't bothered that my father had a mistress. It was *her* mother, my grandmother, that arranged for some mage to curse him. My mother encouraged me to be friendly with my chimeric siblings. I would buy Raquel candy and toys from town and bring them back to her. Her eyes would light up and she would be so happy.

"And then my father finally got his way," Laron whimpered, "and Raquel was gone and I never saw her again." He looked at Sunay, brushing the moisture from his eyes. "Was... was she happy?"

Sunay answered, "As 'appy as anyone can be in an orphanage. But when there's so many around, it can kinda drive ya nutter. She wanted to have 'er own home, live 'er own life rather than steppin' over little bratlings all day. But yer right about 'er, she was always smiling, even when times were rough."

"Thank you, Sunay," he said as he again tried to dry his tears. "But I promised to help you find some mushrooms, did I not? I'm sure I can completely break down in the privacy of my room later."

Sunay didn't give nearly as much distance this time, no more than a handful of yards, nimbly picking morels and truffles while making circles around the considerably less-efficient boy. "Your mother seems like a real piece o' work. I can't imagine bein' so patient with a man who slept around on me, much less accepting 'is bastard kids."

Laron chuckled. "More along the lines of my mother and father marrying out of convenience almost two decades ago, knowing that neither of them really wanted to settle down. As I said, it was my grandmother who got all wound up about fidelity. But my mother *did* believe that every person deserved love and respect. I admire her for that."

"Sounds like a good mother at least."

"Oh, my father is hardly some monster, either," Laron said. "He doesn't *want* to abandon kids on your orphanage's doorstep the minute they emerge from the womb, but keeping them locked away for their entire lives isn't all that great of an option either, especially when you're trying very hard to not remind Parliament that you were a noble once."

Sunay couldn't hide the bitterness in her voice. "Not like we get to roam free *here*."

Laron cringed. "I... suppose that's true. I am sorry, Sunay. I shouldn't presume considering how little I know about the orphanage itself."

He went silent, head down intently, as if a cold stare could force mushrooms out of the earth. Sunay didn't have the heart to tell him that she had already replaced what she needed. She was enjoying talking with someone new for a change, even if she was wasting his time.

Was that selfish?

"How many mushrooms do you need?" He then asked.

Sunay exclaimed, "Oh! Why dontcha bring what you got ta me? I bet between the two o' us, I've got enough to take back without bein' scolded."

He moved to her, pointing a warning finger at Nelly when the dog growled, then presented his backpack to Sunay. The foxgirl analyzed the contents, and got what she figured, maybe four or five usable samples, and a bunch of fungi that would make Kaeli's lips curl and potentially orphans' stomachs to churn.

She dumped all of them into her satchel anyway. She could sort them out later after they parted, and it wouldn't hurt Laron's feelings. "This'll do indeed, boy," she said happily. "Thanks a bunch for 'elpin out!"

Laron wrung his hands, and asked, "Do... do you think we can meet again?"

Sunay cringed. She'd like that, but if Matron Miriam ever found out, she'd probably be skinned alive. "I dunno. It's kinda 'ard to set a meetin' place when I don't know anythin' 'bout what's beyond the forest, and everythin' in the forest probably looks the exact same to ya."

Laron was clearly hurt by that, but it was something Sunay really couldn't do anything about. She didn't like it either. She slung her satchel over her shoulder, and said, "Listen, I gotta go. Our cook is gonna be wantin' these, and she's prob'ly gonna be mad as it is. I'll... see ya... maybe... sometime?"

With that, she dropped to all fours and dashed away, back towards the familiarity of the orphanage, not giving him a chance at parting in case he somehow said something that she'd stupidly agree to. She was so relieved to see the orphanage when she broke through the tree line that she completely forgot to filter out the bad mushrooms that Laron had gathered.

Sunay attempted to do so, but Kaeli noticed her arrival too quickly. "Ey there, Sunay! I was wondering where you were! Hurry up and get those 'shrooms here. The broth is almost completely boiled down!"

And Kaeli immediately identified that Sunay's haul wasn't up to usual standards once the beargirl inspected the haul, "What in the burning pit were you doing out there, girl? You know I can't use these!"

Sunay knew Kaeli was going to demand an explanation, as she hastily composed one based on part of the truth. "I... had to dodge some unwanted company. There were some foxhounds out in the forest, and I had to rush things while shakin' them off my tail."

Kaeli sniffed Sunay's neck. "I thought I smelled something funny. Damn it all, I'm gonna have to tell the matron about this. They're getting closer."

Sunay waved off the idea. "No! It was my fault! I... I... got to close to the outer edge of the forest. I was bein' stupid. There's no reason to panic and worry the matron. She's got enough to worry about as it is."

Kaeli didn't seem entirely convinced by Sunay's explanation, but also acknowledged the foxgirl's reasoning. "Alright... but you make sure you keep close from now on, damn it all. The last thing the orphanage needs are fox hunters tracking your scent here."

"I know! I know!" Sunay insisted. "I promise it won't 'appen again, and I promise ya no 'unters are gonna be trackin' my scent anywhere."

Sunay earnestly believed that.

~ ~ ~

And Sunay turned out to be wrong not even a week later.

"Sunay! Sunay!" Megan called out, dashing around the corner of the orphanage to where Sunay was busy binding some straw into a bale.

It was a fairly important job to get done as they had already lost some straw to rain and the mud that came with it. So Sunay didn't entirely appreciate being interrupted. "What is it? I'm busy."

"The Matron's calling for you, Sunay," Megan explained. "She's not happy."

Sunay scoffed, and said, "She's *never* happy wit' me. That's not new."

"She still wants you in her room. Double time, she says," Megan replied. "I think it has to do with the visitor that came by."

Sunay's ears twitched with worry. The orphanage *never* got visitors. Even people who were trying to hide their chimeras had Matron Miriam come to *them*. "Visitor? Who?"

Megan shrugged, "I don't know. Didn't get the chance to see him. I guess he knocked on the front door, the matron took one look at him, and quickly pushed him into her room. A minute or two later, she sticks her head out the door and screamed your name. I'm surprised you didn't hear it yourself."

Sunay had heard the matron howling, but hadn't paid it much attention. The foxgirl grunted in frustration, and said, "Alright. Tell Kaeli she might have to finish tying up this straw. There ain't too much more to do, but I dunno how long I'll be. All depend on how mad the matron is."

Megan saluted like she was regarding a commanding officer. "Yes, ma'am!"

Sunay rolled her eyes, and shooed off the girl, before taking a slow walk of shame towards the front door of the orphanage. The back door was far closer, but Sunay wanted to delay the coming reprimand as much as possible, even if she didn't even know what she had *done*.

How could she be tied into any 'visitor' that stumbled onto the orphanage? She didn't know anyone outside this damned place.

Except...

Her eyes flared open, and her trudging walk turned into a full sprint. He couldn't have...

She burst through the front door without breaking stride, did the same to Matron Miriam's chambers door, and only came to a full stop once she was a single stride inside.

He could have, and he did.

"Hello, Miss Sunay," Laron said with a cheeky smile, standing proudly in the center of the room.

Matron Miriam was sitting at her desk, hands folded in front of her mouth. She didn't look *enraged* like Megan had implied, but she wasn't happy either. "Sunay, close the door," Miriam ordered quietly.

Sunay glared at Laron as she complied, and the eye contact prompted the matron to say, "I take it you *do* know each other."

"Ma'am, I believe I told you to go easy on her, as our meeting was *my* fault," Laron said, surprising Sunay in how boldly he addressed the matron. No one in the orphanage would get away with talking to her like that.

"You're lucky I don't send you back home with a tanned backside, boy," Miriam snarled.

"Considering what little coin you accept from my father is the reason this orphanage exists, taking liberties with my discipline probably wouldn't be received very well," Laron countered, maintaining his smug expression.

Sunay took three steps to the side, just in case Matron Miriam *could* breath fire like the adults said. She didn't want to be caught in the wake. Unfortunately, that movement turned the matron's gaze on her.

"And you... how did you manage to get so careless?"

Laron interceded again. "I had one of my family's foxhounds with me. Your charge is nimble and sly, but Nelly is not easily thwarted. She was nowhere that the licensed hunters are or had any reason to be. I was on a leisure walk."

Miriam gave him a steely gaze, then said, "I meant how could she lead you *here*. If some nasally soft boy could have followed her scent back here, any of those experienced hunters can as well."

Sunay's ears drooped guiltily. She *had* thought she had hidden her trail well.

"You're forgetting that my father *and* mother know *exactly* where this orphanage is," Laron corrected, "and that my mother has no problem with my associating with chimeras. She wanted to know what happened to Raquel too, after all. Once I showed interest in the orphanage, she gladly yielded the directions how to get here. After all, even the youngest son of the family carries more weight than the lady of the house."

Miriam stiffened at the invocation of the name, and even looked a little guilty. "What do you want, boy?" she finally said tiredly.

"I want to help around the orphanage," Laron declared. "I know you could use the help. I can also offer additional funds and supplies."

"You *want* to fool around with the fox behind you," Miriam countered knowingly. "And even if I felt it was a good match, which I don't, entertaining the idea is *lunacy*."

Laron put a hand to his chest in dismay. "That you would assume a gentleman such as myself to be so base as to pursue a courtship with a lovely young lady he met all of once wounds me!" Seeing Miriam's exaggerated cocked eyebrow, he added, "Of course I would enjoy Miss Sunay's company, but I would *not* be so forward without more time spent in said company."

"I genuinely want to learn more about the people here," Laron continued. "I lost the latter half of Raquel's life. Maybe... I can get to know others. Besides, I doubt *either* of my parents would approve of your embarrassing me by turning me away. Do you honestly think I would be here *without* at least their begrudging permission?"

The matron grunted, "You *are* a right nuisance, that's for sure. All right, for *now*... I'll permit this, if only because appealing to your father would be more trouble than you are. But I swear upon the Coders that made us all, that it wouldn't take much from you to make that trouble worth it. Am I understood?"

Laron smiled in triumph, and bowed deeply. "Yes, ma'am."

Miriam finally pulled her hands away from her face, so she could drop her chin into those same hands tiredly. "Then have Sunay put you to work, and Sunay, don't you *dare* put him to work on what you were doing."

"I've seen 'im try to gather mushrooms. I think I'll start 'im off easy today," Sunay said, keeping her voice grumpy even as inwardly she was going cartwheels. No one had *ever* gotten Matron Miriam to budge on *anything*. "Come along, Laron. I think I know what ya can do."

Sunay led Laron out of Madam Miriam's chamber, and once the door was closed behind them they were nearly swallowed up by a tide of curious chimeras. Sunay understood the curiosity, this was the first new person to cross that threshold in years.

"Hello..." Laron said nervously, not so much out of fear of chimeras as it was they were literally clinging to his legs and thus making it difficult to walk.

"Oi!" Sunay bellowed, shooing the children away and physically prying Andrew off Laron's left leg. "Back off the new guy, will ya? You'll get plenty of chance to get to know 'im."

"He's not a chimera!" Clive said, stating the obvious. "Why is he here? Is he gonna replace the matron?"

That caused a series of worried mumbles to stir across the younger orphans, while the older ones rolled their eyes. Sunay quickly squashed the idea. "He ain't replacin' nobody. He's from outside the forest, and he's gonna be 'elping out here and there."

"Which gets me on point." Sunay said while poking Laron in the chest. "*You* get to entertain the bratlings while *I* finish tying up 'ay bales. Don't thank me, you got the tougher job, I'd bet."

She lingered long enough for the mob to damn near swallow Laron up as he took position in front of the dormant fireplace on the north side of the main room. Hopefully, the novelty would last long enough for her to finish working the straw, and she'd be able to rescue him before the crowd got rowdy.

Kaeli apparently hadn't gotten time to do anything, as everything was as Sunay had left it when she returned to the straw pile. She laid out two long lines of twine on top of a wooden panel, pulled her pitchfork out of the soft earth, then started shoveling straw onto the panel. When she had piled enough, she sorted it out so that it clumped into something roughly resembling a brick, and then tied the two ends of twine together so that the straw would roughly hold that shape over the months that it would be in storage.

Storage was a small shed made from brick that Sunay suspected had once been a sacrificial altar for the church and its alternative practices. Even though Matron Miriam swore there was no way *anyone* would be able to smell anything after decades, Sunay and other chimeras were certain they could smell the remains of burnt human flesh there.

The number of horror stories that could be told about this place entertained the orphans on many a dark, sleepless night.

The shed was nearly full an hour later when Sunay finished the pile that she had been given to work with. Half of it was going to town on Miriam's next trip to trade for supplies, the other half would be used for bedding and patch work over the next few months, just in time for another cartload to arrive to bundle up for the winter months.

She had always wondered why Matron Miriam would bring in a cartload of straw, have Sunay or one of the other older orphans bale it, then take those bales *back* to town, at least until Laron's words put it in perspective. It was one of the ways the noble family assisted the orphanage, no doubt. Have Miriam take straw from the family lands for little or no cost, then sell it in town, taking that profit to purchase more necessary supplies.

It made sense to *her* at least.

Sunay pulled the door to the shed closed with a grunt, flipping the bar that served as a latch around and onto the metal hook that kept it "closed", in the sense that it still left a good two inches of space between the door and the brick wall. That was something she was going to have to fix before foraging animals decided it would make for good food.

Now it was time to see if the bratlings hadn't dismembered Laron in their excitement.

They hadn't, and in fact the kids were actually... *behaving*. The older ones had lost interest in the visitor by the time Sunay returned, having gone back to whatever chores they had been given that day. The younger ones, however, had formed a small semi-circle around where Laron was sitting, looking up at him with beaming smiles as he was engaged in story time.

"And then the Tiger Man jumped off the cliff side, braving the rocks below."

Sunay forced back a chuckle. Laron knew about the Tiger Man. *That* was adorable.

The Tiger Man was a series of stories that Matron Miriam would tell about a "natural" chimera born of a woman who had run away from a horrible father in the long lost land of Scheherazade, and found protection under a spirit of the jungle. Eventually the woman gave birth to a child of great strength and tenacity, and learned to care for *all* people through his mother's lessons.

The Matron often used such stories as teaching tools; for younger kids, there were stories that taught basic compassion and the good in people's hearts. As the orphans grew older, the stories became more complex, featuring the Tiger Man's own fights with equality, as well as more negative emotions like how to handle his own anger and rage.

Laron was telling a tale that none of them had heard yet.

"Did the Tiger Man make it?" Clive asked, his eyes wide with worry.

"No one knows," Laron answered. "He was never seen after that final hunt. But the Tiger Man was strong and bold. Tales say that when he's needed, he'll come back."

Not the best lesson to teach the bratlings, Sunay thought. There were *plenty* of times the chimera's hero had been needed. But at the same time, the little ones didn't seem traumatized by the story.

"I bet the Tiger Man helps people of the Line take chimeras to new homes when they're all grown up!" Artemis said hopefully.

"He might," Laron said. "The Tiger Man is as mysterious as he is powerful. There's little knowing where he could be at any given time." He then caught Sunay's gaze. "Oh, greetings Miss Sunay. I take it you've finished your tasks. What time is it?"

"Evening's breaking, if you have somewhere to be," she said.

Laron grimaced. "I do, in fact, and I did not bring a horse with me. I'll have to do so in the future I think."

There were immediate protests from his audience. "I'll be back, little ones, I promise! But sadly, I have other responsibilities and a family that *would* get concerned if I'm gone all night."

Matron Miriam took that moment to interject. "And just when will you be back, young man?"

"Well, I have my tutoring for the next two days, but I have a day free to volunteer after that. Would that be acceptable, ma'am?"

The normally gruff matron was trying really hard not to sound *too* pleased. Even she had to admit that Laron had kept the bratlings out of everyone else's way. "Well, what do the little ones think? Would that be acceptable?"

The reply was loud and in unison. "YES!"

"Then it is settled, we will see you in three days, young man." The matron regarded Sunay, and with a tired sigh said, "Sunay, escort the boy back to the main road, but *do* take care that you aren't seen."

"Yes, ma'am," Sunay said, flipping her right hand, beckoning Laron to follow her. "Come on, boy. Best to get ya back 'ome before yer parents git worried."

Laron complied, falling in step behind her and following through the front doors, nodding in parting to the older orphans still milling about on their chores, and through the clearing into the forest proper.

"I can't believe that worked," Laron finally admitted once he felt they were safely out of earshot of anyone who could hear.

Sunay was confused. "What worked?"

"Bluffing my way into helping out here."

Sunay's eyes bulged in fright, and forced herself to keep her voice down. "You... you *lied?*"

"Well, not *entirely.* I told my parents I'm volunteering some of my time to the church. Which I *am*, they just don't know that it's Matron Miriam," he said, biting his lower lip. "I snuck into my father's study and learned the directions to the orphanage. My mother probably *would* have told me, but I didn't want to get her in trouble."

"Your dad is gonna flay you alive if he finds out!"

"My father only cares that I am home by sundown. He has enough matters to deal with and two older sons to manage. My mother is going to be concerned, but she'll support my initiative here, if she even bothers to ask. Almost can't believe that I'd thank the Coders for inattentive parents."

Sunay shook her head in disbelief. "You really wanna spend time wit' me that bad, eh?"

"I've lived my entire life without a purpose. I'm the kid they're going to ship off to some church duty anyway once I come of age so that I don't get any ideas of inheriting any of the family land. Those little kids smiling when they see me, listening to me tell dumb stories... it reminded me of how Raquel would get so very happy to see me. It felt good."

He tenderly grasped the back of Sunay's hand, and added, "But I certainly won't protest to spending more time with a pretty girl like you."

She flattened her ears distastefully, even as her cheeks betrayed the compliment. "Oh, you hush."

The pair stopped just short of where the tree line broke. "I probably should listen to the matron for once, so this is as far as I go," Sunay said in parting. "You promise yer comin' back?"

"In three days time," Laron acknowledged. "I'd return sooner if I didn't have tutoring to attend to."

Sunay then raised herself onto her toes, dropping a shy peck on Laron's cheek. "Well, there's something for you to think about while yer waitin'. Ta ta, boy."

This time she scampered at top speed simply so that she could explain the flush on her face by running so fast back to the orphanage. Maybe Matron Miriam thought entertaining affections for the young man was a bad idea. Burning pits, even *she* thought it was a bad idea.

But did it really hurt to dream?

# Chapter Three: Over the River and Through the Woods

Laron didn't help Sunay's conflicted emotions in the slightest. As summer yielded to fall, the young nobleman had been spending at least two days a week at the orphanage, entertaining the bratlings and even helping Kaeli in the kitchen. He had offered to help with more difficult and potentially dangerous manual labor (like the repairs Sunay frequently performed), but there was only so far Matron Miriam was going to bend, especially since she was justifiably terrified about what would happen were Laron to injure himself.

And in that same stretch, he made his interest in Sunay painfully clear, much to Miriam's dismay. Sunay herself gave lip service to Miriam's reservations, even as the foxgirl reveled in the attention of such a dashing and sophisticated gentleman. Sunay still didn't think it was a good idea, mind, but at the same time what healthy young lady *wouldn't* swoon a little at her own personal fairy-tale prince?

"Would you like to have lunch with me in town tomorrow?" he whispered in her ear.

Sunay nearly slammed her hammer down on her thumb with how the question completely broke her concentration. The first emotion that stirred after her brain caught up was anger. "Coders, boy! That is *not* a question ya ask a girl when she's tryin' to fix a wall!"

She then whirled about to face him and his broadly grinning face. "And what in the Coders' holy names makes ya think it's a good idea to take... mmph?"

"Keep your voice down!" Laron warned as he slapped his hand over her mouth, then smirked at her hysterical response when he pulled away. "Do you *honestly* thinks that you'll be set to the stake the minute you step outside the forest?"

"Uhhh... yes?"

He shook his head in disbelief. "Believe it or not, the people of this area tend to have a very 'live and let live' attitude when it comes to nobles, and the bastard children that came from those nobles. You would be *more* than able to blend in with the rest of the outside world. The tail might take a little creativity..."

"It don't matter, 'cause the matron would never allow it!"

Laron rolled his eyes. "That's why you *don't tell her*, girl. I've seen you gather mushrooms, it normally takes you thirty minutes, and then you spend the rest of the day napping in the woods." He then grinned cheekily and added, "or lately fooling around with me. Instead of napping, you meet me and we go into town for lunch."

Sunay blushed so red it almost covered her freckles. "Say I agree to this crazy idea. You're not even *here* tomorrow."

"That's *why* we go tomorrow. I won't be here, so no one will suspect you're fooling around outside of the forest. Come on, do you honestly want to stay cooped up in this clearing all your life?"

Of *course* she didn't want to be secluded in this orphanage all her life. "But..."

"If your answer to every potential danger was to hide from it, you'd never leave your bed, and frankly I've seen your bed. You really need to assert a little independence once in a while. Otherwise, you'll wind up a simpering ninny doing whatever you can to endear yourself to your parents in the hope you'll get a little slice of inheritance like the second son in my family. Coders, is *that* boy a right mess. You don't even have *that* to try and preserve."

He took Sunay's hands, the hammer dropping lifeless from her fingers as she caught his gaze, and those bright blue eyes that she swore glimmered like sapphires. "Sunay, I want to show you *my* world, and I want to do it before we're too old and gray to care about being caught."

There was no use trying to resist. At that point, she was putty in his hands, and she knew it. "Oh... alright. But 'ow are we goin' to pull this off?"

"We'll meet at the brook rock tomorrow at noon," Laron said, referring to the large granite rock that they had found last month while on one of their mushroom hunts, that rested along a small tributary that ran through the southwest portion of the forest. It was a solid landmark for them to meet illicitly. "From there, I can take us into town. I know exactly where to go, too. I bet you haven't had a good hunk of meat since you were born."

Sunay had to lick her lips to keep from salivating at the idea. She knew foxes were carnivorous by nature, but that portion of her diet had to be limited due to the number of chimeras cursed with herbivorous forms that found meat inherently distasteful. And what meaty samples she *could* get were generally of poor quality. "Then it's..."

"A date. Yes," Laron said with a wink. "But for now you should probably pick up that hammer and finish repairing the wall here.

I think Matron Miriam is gonna start to wonder why you stopped, and will probably blame it on my boyish charms. I wouldn't blame her if that's the case, I do have such very kissable lips."

Again, Sunay blushed, and she pushed him away while trying to hide it. "Then get outta here so I can work!"

That loud protest drew Matron Miriam's attention, who threw open her door and stuck her head around the corner. "Laron! You're here to work, not flirt! If you can't find something to do that doesn't involve Sunay, *I'll* find something for you, and I promise you *won't* like it!"

The little ones playing in the main hall started giggling at the matron's reprimand, and Laron backed away as if chided, even though he flashed Sunay a knowing grin. "Understood, ma'am. I do apologize. Come along, little ones, I think I know of another game I can teach you."

The children cheered, and Sunay smiled warmly while trying to control her rampant color that had spread to her neck. That distraction allowed Kaeli to sneak up her, something that the beargirl should *never* be able to do.

"Is little Sunay about to be very *naughty?*" Kaeli asked playfully, startling the foxgirl into dropping her hammer again.

Scrambling to pick it up again, Sunay's attempt to hide her guilt was terribly transparent. "I... I dunno what yer talkin' about."

"Ol' Kaeli has some good ears. Your boy there is pretty clever, but it'll be a frozen day here before two kids pull the rug over my eyes."

Sunay's ears dropped in defeat. "Ya... yer not gonna tell the matron, are ya? If'n I don't go?"

Instead, Kaeli bellowed, "Matron, I need to borrow Sunay for a minute! I'll send her right back to patching the wall when I'm done!" Then with a softer, conspiratorial tone, she beckoned Sunay with a finger. "Follow me."

Kaeli's kitchen was always a warm welcome place, filled with wonderful smells that made tummies rumble. It was also a safe place where the Matron Miriam didn't readily go unlike any other room in the orphanage. Which was a good thing, because Kaeli had some things to say that would likely make the matron flush with anger.

"I was ten when the Revolution started. I was eleven when the conflict spread to this part of the republic. I was thirteen by the time I found my way to this orphanage. Up until that point, I could walk freely in the streets of Navarre. I'd be glared at to be sure, occasionally threatened for being a bastard noble's girl, but I could walk freely.

"It doesn't bother me that I can't anymore, because I'm a homebody. I like settling in one place. It's why I'm still here while everyone else my age has *long* since tried their hand with the open world. But you, Sunay, you're an explorer. You want to see the world out there, and you should get the chance. You should see the streets that I walked down, see how they've changed, *if* they've changed."

Sunay's eyes had narrowed to dots, and her jaw hung loose from the rest of her head. Was this real?

Kaeli turned to her left, and pulled a long black box from the top of her meager spice cabinet. "Your boy isn't wrong. You certainly could pass off as a completely normal human with just a little bit of work. Here. I've been sewing this together in my spare time figuring this day would come eventually."

Sunay took the box with trepidation, giving Kaeli large, questioning, eyes.

"Go on, child. Open it up."

When the foxgirl finally complied and lifted the lid, she was greeted with blouse, skirt, and a hat. The blouse was completely normal, dyed in a pastel green which matched the skirt. Sunay hadn't worn many skirts, as they didn't allow the freedom of movement she needed to do chores, so she was uncertain about it even before discovering it was long enough for her to trip over if she took too large of a stride.

Kaeli then took the hat, a brown, floppy... thing... and put it on Sunay's head so that the loose top draped down the back of her hair, then patted down the foxgirl's ears. "You'll have to keep your ears down for it to look right, as well as be careful not to run too fast. But I think you'll manage just fine."

Sunay tried not to cry. She failed.

"Now, now... no tears. I don't think you'll be running away tomorrow," Kaeli said soothingly. "Or at least... you better not. Enjoy the outside world. Let the rest come in time."

Sunay still could manage to find words thanks to the lump in her throat, so the foxgirl resorted to dropping the box and enveloping Kaeli in a happy hug.

The beargirl chuckled. "Awww... you're just the sweetest thing when you want to be. Now get back to work. I'll leave the box on top of the spice cabinet, and you can grab it when you leave in the morning."

~ ~ ~

Sunay followed those instructions the following morning, though the foxgirl *did* insist on gathering the mushrooms she was allegedly heading out to fetch, even as Kaeli insisted it wasn't necessary. With the black box under her arm, she spent the time before the meeting gathering, and left the satchel hanging from a tree to keep animals from getting into it while she was in town.

And even then she arrived at the meeting spot too early. By the time that she had changed, stuffed the box with her old clothes into her pack and secured the whole lot in the trees, the sun hadn't even reached the treetops. She then scaled the five foot rock and settled onto the flat top, a surface that allowed just enough room for two teenagers to sit *very* close. She crossed her legs, dropped her elbows onto her knees, and her head onto her hands. She then exhaled with a puttering sound of exasperation.

This was going to be one *boring* wait...

It was no more than half an hour before she first heard the swishing sound of someone hacking through the underbrush, a fairly common behavior of hunters trying to clear fox holes. Sunay immediately vacated her position on the rock, instead using it as a hiding spot from the slowly approaching noise.

The sound stopped as her sense of smell kicked in, which eased her concern and caused her to smile and her heart to do flip-flops. It was a very familiar, very welcome smell, and Sunay broke from her hiding place, and moved as swiftly as she could in her skirt towards her object of affection.

As a result, she couldn't engage in the flying tackle that she would have wanted to do, instead waiting for Laron as he appeared through the trees, sheathing a broad machete that he had been using to clear a path through the taller weeds.

He saw her soon after, and gave her his familiar warm, lopsided grin. "I see I wasn't the only one eager to get a start on the day."

Sunay tried to say something, but the words failed to form in her throat, so she settled for a breathless giggle as his arms circled comfortably around her waist. This had become a familiar feeling, as did the loving, open mouthed kiss they shared a breath later.

She was flushed by the time they parted, and that color only built as he looked down through the v-neck of her blouse and said, "You look very nice."

"Kaeli made it," Sunay answered. "She said I should blend in jus' fine."

Laron nodded in confirmation. "Might wonder why a girl would be wearing such an old style, but since I don't think anyone is going to think you're some daughter of a wealthy family it certainly won't raise any questions."

Sunay pushed the young man away, dropped her hands on her hips, and shot him a dark expression. "Are you sayin' I don't look sophisticated? Ya think I can't pull it off?"

Laron didn't rise to the bait, and simply replied, "No, but that's one of the reasons I like you."

Sunay's lips twitched into a grin, even as her eyes narrowed. "Kaeli's right. You *are* a clever boy."

"I do try." He then gestured behind him, and said, "Would you like to make our way to town, my lady? I have cleared the path for you so as not to soil your wonderful clothes."

He offered his arm, and Sunay slipped hers in the crook of his elbow. "And such a gentleman too."

Sunay knew the forest surrounding Matron Miriam's orphanage pretty well, which was also how she knew she was getting into the areas she hadn't explored often. The nerves steadily built as they moved still further from comfortable environs, to the point that she was clinging to Laron's arm as if she would fall up into the open sky as the tree line thinned.

Laron asked, "You've never been this far away from home, have you?"

"Once," Sunay admitted. "When I was nine. Got all the way to the treeline when Matron Miriam found me. She beat my 'ind end good fer that one. I know she was tryin' to protect me, I understan' that there are people out in this world that would love to see me burn... but at the time I was so sore at 'er."

"Well... then I'd say take a look now, because the world lies before you."

Sure enough, the trees were now behind her, and said world felt even bigger than what Matron Miriam taught in her lessons. The grasslands extended to the south and a slow decline towards what she had been told was sandy coastline, and to the north... mountains. Real *mountains*, with peaks dusted with a white patches of snow. Sunay had been able to see the base of that mountain range from as far as she dared walk down the clearing road, but not much else.

She broke away from Laron, drinking in the unobstructed view for the first time she could clearly remember. It was amazing.

She wanted to go everywhere she could see all at once. From that breathtaking panorama, the sight of the town of Navarre didn't hold quite as much interest anymore.

The town commanded the immediate view, stretching across her vision from north to south, with farms growing grain and grazing cattle to the north side, yielding to small wood houses and cabins clustered together before the brick and mortar streets and buildings of the town square. Further west, along a gentle incline, was a genuine castle, with an exterior wall and two square, buttressed towers.

Laron followed Sunay's line of sight, and said, "Take a guess where my family lives. I'll give you an up close look later. Let's get on the road... we don't blend in very well off the beaten path."

The road itself was nearby, and much more maintained than the worn path of dirt that was the orphanage's excuse for a "road." This was made of cobblestone and moved to the north, as if giving the forest where Miriam's orphanage was hidden away a wide berth.

"Navarre is actually a bit off the beaten path," Laron explained. "This area used to be a resort area for royalty and higher ranking nobles. Good hunting, beaches, mild in the winter when the northern part of the kingdom like Caravel was buried under inches of snow."

Sunay's attention was stolen by the cacophony of hoof beats originating from a four horse cart, drawing a high bedded cart with wheels taller than she was. She had thought Patrona, the horse that led Miriam's cart was big. This cart could have carried enough supplies in a single trip to maintain the orphanage for a year.

"I wouldn't look *quite* so amazed, Sunay," Laron whispered as the cart quickly passed them on its path into the town, "considering if anyone asks, you're a merchant's daughter from Lourdis."

"Lourdis?" Sunay asked, her voice drifting off. She couldn't rightly explain why, but that name sounded familiar.

"It's a bit to the south, and about two days travel to the east. It's the major trading post in Avalon before the Great Trade Line heads north towards Caravel. This road here is just a minor branch off that major trade path. If anyone asks, just make up something about the Merchant's Guild, and that you rarely had time outside of the Trade District to really mull about."

Sunay pursed her lips thoughtfully, trying to absorb that information.

"I highly doubt you'll have to make small talk of that nature with anybody, but it doesn't hurt to be prepared. For the most part, if you act really shy and let me do the talking, I doubt anyone will even ask your name."

Sunay could do shy. She discovered that much simply because she had started to cling to Laron's arm again because the increase in people had equally increased her nerves. She had never *seen* so many people in one place before. Laron patted her hand comfortably, smiling in amusement at her skittish behavior. The foxgirl glared at him, then gave a sneer that betrayed a hint of her unusually long canine teeth.

The town boundary was a fairly stark transition, as the brick and stone took over and the grass nigh entirely yielded. Even if the brick was a drab gray, it was still exhilarating to see the remarkable construction as opposed to the molding wood, tar, and thatch that kept her home together. The sense of wonder once again overcame Sunay's uncertainties, and she marveled at the buildings with their colorful banners and signs indicating taverns, bakeries, tailors, a blacksmith...

"What's a massage parlor?" Sunay asked, pointing at a red and white sign hanging in front of the peculiarly named "Madame Julia's Massage Parlor." She had heard of the other shops before, but that was a new one.

This time, Laron blushed all the way down to his neck, and he coughed nervously. "Best not to worry about *that*, my dear."

"But... I wanna *see!*" Sunay insisted.

"No. You really don't. Besides, it's not open."

"Why not?"

"It only serves... customers... later at night."

"Why would it do that?"

Their conversation was interrupted by a pair of old men, lounging at a circular table in front of one of the taverns to Sunay's right, sipping golden brown beer from crystal clear mugs. "That's what brothels in Avalon started calling themselves to avoid being investigated by the Republican Police," the first said, a scrawny, shriveled up specimen with about half the required number of teeth and only strands remaining of a full head of hair.

The second didn't look quite as weathered by time and age, with a ring of silver hair around his head and something resembling meat on his bones, but his tone was just as leery, and sent shivers down Sunay's spine. "I'm rather surprised that no one's ever asked a pretty little thing like you to work there."

Sunay *knew* what a brothel was, as well as the implication of the mens' words, especially as both mens' line of sight were blatantly drawn directly at Sunay's chest. Disgust shifted to anger quickly. "Why I oughta," she snarled angrily, and lunged forward a stride before Laron stopped her with a hand around her wrist.

"Sunay, dearie. Don't waste your breath or your fists. Those two aren't worth it."

"Ha! I thought you looked familiar, Laron!" the second man said in jeering tease. "So what is this about, eh? Trying to get some fun in before you get shipped off to the church, are you?"

Laron's lips pursed into a tight line, and Sunay couldn't remember the young man *ever* looking that annoyed. "Being sent to the church would no doubt be a better fate than what Marie would do if she learned you were here rather than at the fishing hole, Mister Henry."

That got the second man to snap his mouth shut and his eyes to narrow, and successfully turned the jovial ire of the first man on him. Laron took the opportunity to lead Sunay forward, leaving the two old men to bicker amongst themselves. "Come along, dear. I think you need some food."

She did, actually. A breakfast of oatmeal hadn't set terribly well, as dreams of meat had invaded her thoughts since Laron put the idea in her head yesterday. "Yes. Food would be very good."

Laron guided her to their left, onto a street heading south, with a cobbler shop, an inn, and a large farmer's market with carts loaded with vegetables and bundles of grain to her left. To her right, a butcher's brick and mortar shop wafted smells of beef and poultry, followed by a smokehouse next to it with fish and salts.

"Patience. While I'm sure getting the product straight from the source would probably be cheaper, part of the goal here is that we *don't* have to cook it ourselves."

Sunay stopped, discovering that she had unconsciously been leaning towards the butcher's shop with each step and dragging Laron with her. She smiled guiltily, and patted Laron's hand while she allowed him to guide her back towards the market street.

Past that market was their destination, another gray brick square building, this one with a blue and white awning proclaiming the name of "Louis' Gourmet Cuisine" that covered an exterior dining space enclosed by an elaborate iron fence with ribbed iron bars four feet high that crossed over and around each other and tipped to points. The enclosure itself was well populated, with half of the tables already occupied with couples and even three families of at least six people.

There was an open door in the fence, made from the same

material and pattern, that allowed Sunay and Laron entry, and stepping under the awning prompted a man dressed neatly in long black slacks and a frilled white button up shirt to emerge from the interior.

"Welcome, my friends, to Louis' Gourmet Cuisine," the waiter said with a thick accent, drawing his vowels long and seeming to cut sounds short of what Sunay expected. "Ah, Master Laron, I see you have an elegant young lady with you today. Could I recommend dining in the open this day? It looks splendid for autumn."

Laron returned the courtesy. "That *was* our intent, good man. Thank you. Perhaps something on the edge so that the lady can have a good view."

The waiter bowed deeply, and said, "Then I know the perfect place. Do follow me, sir and madam."

He led Sunay and Laron to the southwest corner and an open table located right at that location. "Do you need a menu, or do you know what you wish to order?"

Laron nodded, and locked eyes with Sunay. "I think we'll have something simple today, good man. A garden salad with Aramathean dressing for two, and then two pound sirloin, one well cooked..." then with a knowing wink to Sunay, "and one rare."

"Any drinks today, sir?"

"How is the lemonade today?"

The waiter sounded almost offended. "Excellent as always, young master."

"We'll take a pitcher and two glasses, then."

"Splendid choice, my friends. I shall return shortly."

Despite the fact that there were people all around, and even one woman sitting behind Sunay that was so close that the foxgirl's nose curled from the intensity of her rose perfume, their location *felt* intimate and private. The fence might as well have been a castle wall even as it offered a spectacular view of the South Forever Sea in the distance. It was something just short of magical.

If this was how normal people always lived, she didn't *ever* want to go back to the orphanage, even if she risked being burned at the stake.

The waiter returned with their glasses, filled with a pale yellow liquid. She knew what lemons were, as Kaeli was known to use lemon peels as a seasoning, and as such was wary that the sour fruit could make for a good drink. But Laron seemed to enjoy it, and Sunay *was* supposed to blend in.

And she learned something new, that lemons *could* be

something tasty... tart yet sweet on the tongue, the bite becoming more mild with each sip. She had drank half the glass before realizing that Laron had stopped after that first sip, the cheerful face he had put on dropping to reveal a glum frown and downcast eyes.

She instantly was concerned. Laron *never* looked this gloomy. She set down her glass, reached out to touch his hand. "Oi," she asked, "what's wrong?"

His happy mask popped back into place as their waiter appeared again, presenting a wide lipped bowl with salad, a small cup filled with a light amber oil, and two pristine white porcelain plates. Laron divided the greens and explained, "Well, it ties in with what one of those old coots said earlier. My father confirmed that I'm being sent to the monastery in Delhomme next spring. I knew that he would, of course, but that still doesn't make the news any easier."

Laron had talked about this before, though usually in far off terms. She also knew he really *didn't* want to be a part of the Coders' Truth Church, which had become the dominant denomination in Avalon.

"Would that *really* be so bad?" she asked.

"Considering the Truth Church is the one with the open bounty on people like..." he stopped himself before referring specifically to Sunay, "chimeras, yes, it *would* be that bad. My father doesn't get it. It has *nothing* to do with an inheritance. He can give me *nothing* for all I care, but I refuse to be an ordained member of that hateful place."

Sunay confirmed Laron's opinion. "I don't blame ya. I wouldn't either."

Laron shook off the doldrums, and forced a smile that Sunay would have thought was genuine if she didn't know better by now. "Oh, don't mind my upper class problems. This is supposed to be about you!"

"About *us,*" Sunay insisted with a grin.

Laron conceded the point. "Very well. About *us*."

He tapped Sunay's glass with the rim of his, took a drink, then began eating along with Sunay. The salad wasn't bad, even if the oily dressing didn't suit the foxgirl's tongue well, but it wasn't meat. She was promised *meat*. Real juicy tender *meat*.

The girl would at last get her desires with another visit from their waiter. It was everything she dreamed of, another immaculately white plate with one thick slab of meaty goodness, with a light brown and gray grilled surface dusted with pepper, salt, and a pungent spice she had never smelled before. And inside... tender, red muscle tissue that leaked bloody juice.

About the only way that steak could be any more fresh was if the waiter had brought out the cow for Sunay to kill herself. She knew she was drooling, and couldn't help it.

"So... are you going to eat it or admire it all day?" Laron teased.

"Hush," Sunay huffed. "This is beautiful."

"Well, bear in mind that I *do* have a curfew."

Sunay glared at him, and very deliberately grabbed her knife and fork, cutting off a large bite and chewing animatedly.

"Good girl," he said with a light-hearted laugh, one that Sunay could tell was legitimate, and caused her to crack a smile.

They ate in silence again, Laron stealing glances at Sunay, his expression slowly turning serious with each meeting of their eyes. Halfway through his steak, he slowed his eating to continue conversation. "I have friends of the family in Aramathea."

"Hmm?" Sunay mumbled, mercifully remembering the matron's lessons about proper manners that forbid a person from trying to talk with their mouth full.

"I'm not going to the church. By the next spring, I'll leave home and leave the Republic."

Sunay swallowed quickly, coughing once because the bite was a little larger than she had expected. "Your family will let you do that?"

Laron scoffed. "They can't stop me. I'm of legal age of adulthood as it is. I have my own papers of travel that do not require my father or mother's blessing. I could walk straight to the border camp, walk straight through, and into the Free Provinces separating the two empires without even the slightest worry. Even *if* my father would be interested in pursuing me, he wouldn't have the clout to influence the Republican Police way out there."

Sunay was interested in what Laron was saying, but the steak was so good. She had to finish swallowing before she could speak again. "And the friends in Aramathea come in... how?"

"Well, they can speak for me when I reach the empire's border, as well as provide me with work and assistance while I'm there. I'm not some worthless noble's boy who never learned a trade. I know economics. I know how to trade and negotiate. It might not be easy, but I can make it, and even if I can't it will because of *my* failures."

"You're a lot braver than anyone gives ya credit for, aren'tcha?"

"I like to think so."

He resumed eating, although Sunay had finished before he was even halfway done. He continued stealing glances at her, his eyes thoughtful, as if silently contemplating something that he wasn't sure how to ask. As she was preparing to ask what was on his mind, they were interrupted one more time by their waiter. "Would the sir and madam like dessert this day?"

"Whatcha got?" Sunay asked, the idea of sweets almost as tantalizing as thoughts of meat.

"We have spiced apple pastries, chocolate filled crepes, and a vanilla crème pudding."

"Yes!"

The waiter blinked, and queried, "To..."

Sunay couldn't understand the confusion. "The lot."

Their waiter gave Laron a silent, questioning look, and the young man deferred with a palms up gesture towards Sunay and a smile. "Very well, madam. I will be right back."

Dessert was delicious, even if Laron barely sampled the treats that had been ordered. He paid the bill in secret, refusing to show Sunay just how much she had cost him, even when she threatened to punch him. Instead, he led her to the west side of town, towards his family castle.

"I suppose that *is* technically correct," Laron said when Sunay referred to it as such. "Though it pales in comparison to some of the grand castles in larger cities. Don't get me mistaken, it certainly is a luxurious place to live, but when I think of castles, I tend to think of something else."

They followed the road on the west side of town, about a mile from that castle, following Laron's arm as he pointed towards the southern tower. "My room is right on the third level of that tower. I get such a wonderful view of the sea. I honestly think outside of my family, that's the thing I'm going to miss the most."

He stopped abruptly, and Sunay nearly tripped trying to keep to his side. "But there's one thing I don't want to miss," he said, allowing himself to catch her eyes.

Sunay quickly got what he meant, and her eyes widened fearfully. She couldn't speak, every single muscle in her body had frozen.

Laron took her limp hands, and said, "Sunay, I want you to come with me. I know this is sudden, and I know we haven't known each other very long... but you deserve a better life than that orphanage, and I think I can give it to you."

The foxgirl managed to get her mouth working at the very least, not that she offered much. "But..."

"I can have papers of travel made for you easily enough. Once you're in the Free Provinces, there'll be no need to hide who you are, and once at the Aramathean border you can plead for amnesty. As a chimera, and knowing what our land does to your kind, there's no reason it wouldn't be granted."

"But..."

"This isn't a decision you have to make right away," Laron said. "I'm not going anywhere until winter at the very earliest. It's a decision I *know* you will be nervous and scared about. But *please* think about it."

Sunay was finally able to string words together. "I... I will." Sure, it wasn't *many* words, but it was a start.

He leaned in to kiss her, then pulled up just before contact, his attention focusing on something over her left shoulder. "Oh dear... this is unexpected."

"What is?" Sunay asking, first turning her head, then the rest of her body when that wasn't enough to get a look at what was going on behind her. A large caravan of three wagons, each pulled by two snow white horses, was crossing the road junction behind her, heading west towards Laron's family castle. The wagons were far more elaborate than she had ever seen, covered with royal blue awnings with silver trim, and pearl sides with glass-covered windows and a door with brass handles.

At the rear of each cart a sign hung, bearing a crest of a winding blue serpent on a white wield, followed by three blue striped flags. "What is *that?*" the foxgirl said with curiosity.

"That is a train from Snake River," Laron explained, his voice void of any emotion. "And judging from the banners, it's an envoy carrying the Dog of the Republic, Cavalier Norman."

"The Dog of the Republic?"

"Cavalier Norman, as his title suggests, was a knight of the kingdom before the Revolution. Considering his staunch moral beliefs and championing of the church, it should have been little surprise that he would turn on the philandering and corrupt crown when the upheaval finally came. He earned his current title because the Republic sends him to ferret out and investigate rumors pertaining to the royal family and deposed nobility that supported them."

"Is that bad?"

Laron shook his head, and said, “Inconvenient, perhaps. My father is going to be on his absolute best behavior, but the royal family is dead, no matter what rumors linger about Princess Viola, and all the major Royalists went *north* for sanctuary, not south.”

“Viola...” Sunay whispered. That name *sounded* familiar, but she couldn't figure out from where. She didn't know anybody by that name.

“She was the youngest child of King George, and rumor has it that she somehow fled before the Revolution, which doesn't make one whit of sense. A princess doesn't just disappear.” The young man sighed forlornly. “However, I'm afraid this means I'm going to have to cut our date shorter than I wanted. My father is going to want the entire family present to entertain our visitors.”

“Oh,” Sunay replied sadly. “Well... I should be goin' then, eh?”

Laron flashed a smile. “It would *not* be gentlemanly to leave a woman unattended in a strange town.” He began walking again, towards the intersection that the caravan had passed through, and turning the opposite direction, heading east back in the general direction of the forest and the orphanage.

On that return trip, Laron said, “I will probably miss my visit to the orphanage tomorrow. But I promise I'll be back one the first day of the new week.”

“Okay,” Sunay said distractedly. She had been looking forward to that visit, but she forced herself to understand that sometimes, even noble men had obligations and duties they couldn't shirk.

The foxgirl grasped Laron's hand as they slipped back into the cover of the forest, back towards their meeting rock. Once there, he spun her about into his arms, kissed her soundly, and removed her hat. “You don't need this silly thing anymore,” he said with a smile, one that quickly dissolved back into the glumly thoughtful expression that bothered her.

“Now what?” Sunay asked.

“You're a *red* fox chimera. I just noticed that,” he replied, clearly distracted.

“Yah. And?”

“The gray is the dominant fox in this part of Avalon. The red... is more common to the north.”

Sunay grumbled in annoyance. “I came from the north, so that kinda makes sense, dontcha think? What about it?”

Laron flashed another fake smile, and stepped away, giving

her back the hat. "Nothing, I'm sure. Just silly me having silly thoughts that assuredly mean nothing. I tend to do that."

That wasn't much of an answer, but she probably wasn't going to get a better one without a fight, and she didn't want to soil the dress Kaeli made. "That you do."

Laron shook his head clear of his thoughts, and reached into his pocket. "I have one last thing for you. A gift I want you to have."

The young man presented a small red leather box, which Sunay opened to reveal a single oval sky blue earring with two small jewels of the same vivid light blue color hanging from a silver thread off the bottom, and all connected to a gold hook on the top.

Sunay gasped, and said, "Laron... it's beautiful..."

"I'm saving the other earring for if you decide to come with me," he said cheekily. "Consider it added... incentive."

Laron parted quickly after one more hasty kiss on her cheek, leaving Sunay to get her pack out of the tree she had hung it from, change to her regular clothes while sticking the earring into the left pocket of her trousers, and return to the orphanage.

If she seemed distracted, no one back at the orphanage asked her about it; which was a good thing considering she probably wouldn't have been able to provide a good answer with all the thoughts swimming in her head.

Things that she felt like she should know but had no idea how, or why she felt guilty that she didn't... names that she swore she never heard before, yet somehow were familiar... wrapping around snippets of dreams she could barely remember, a hazy recollection of things that might have happened when she was too young to really understand... and one request that hung over them all, a very real thing that she could recall vividly.

*"By the next spring, I will leave home and leave the Republic."*

*"Sunay, I want you to come with me."*

Those words haunted her even as she curled up on her bed of straw to sleep. Now that she had seen the outside world, it was so painful to come back to this wretched mess, and those thoughts made Sunay feel like a terrible person.

*"You're not going to leave, are you, Sunay?"*

Sunay didn't even want to answer that question to herself, because deep down she knew what her answer would be, and that it would break Matron Miriam's heart.

## Chapter Four: Chosen

Laron, as expected, didn't show up at the time he was supposed to, and Sunay found it ironic that despite all the snarling and complaining Matron Miriam had about him being here to begin with that she would get so very annoyed when he didn't show up. Sunay had to pretend that she didn't know why, and the deception made her feel worse than she already did concerning what was churning in her heart.

Two days after that, however, there was no need for deception.

It was the start of a new week, and Laron *still* hadn't come back.

*Now* Sunay was concerned, and she went into action right after breakfast and Matron Miriam's prayer session. She entered the kitchen, took the dress box off of the spice cabinet, and explained to a questioning Kaeli, "Somethin's wrong. Laron should have come by."

Kaeli warned, "Sunay, it's one thing to roam about the outside world with a guide. It's entirely another to go out on your own."

"I know that. I'm scared witless that I'll do somethin' stupid and get caught. But... this isn't like Laron. He doesn't go back on his word, and he gave me his word. Somethin's not right."

"And if there is? What do you expect to do about it?"

Sunay set her jaw in the face of Kaeli's protests. "I dunno. It'll depend on *what* is wrong. I'm not gonna charge in stupidly and start attackin' people, if that's what yer worried about."

Kaeli really didn't want to agree; Sunay could see it in the beargirl's eyes and how her cheeks trembled.

"It's probably even nothin'... there were guests from another town that came by yesterday, and they're probably still lingerin' about," Sunay added, and once she remembered that it *did* seem the most likely explanation. But at the same time... the most likely explanation didn't *feel* right.

Kaeli picked up on that too. "You don't think that's it, do you?"

"Nope. But if it makes you any less freaked, I'll take it."

The older woman finally relented. "Just... please please *please*... don't do anything stupid. Find out what's happened, and get back home as fast as you can, alright?"

"I will."

Kaeli stepped aside, allowing Sunay access to the back door, which the foxgirl burst out of at a sprint, diving into the cover of the woods in seconds.

Stopping at the meeting stone to change, Sunay decided as she was pulling off her belt to merely pull her skirt *over* her trousers, and leave the blouse behind. She wanted to save time, and if she needed to move quickly for whatever reason, then she could just rip the skirt off and haul tail.

The path that Laron cleared earlier came of benefit, as it hadn't grown over in the last three days, giving Sunay an easily traversable path out of the forest and to the outskirts of Navarre.

Even for the late morning, the town seemed lifeless. The travelers on the road were uneasy, and the bulk were going *away* from the town, rather than *toward* it. Curiosity wanted her to ask about the exodus, but fear kept her from talking with people and possibly revealing ignorance of things she should know.

Two of the covered carts from the caravan that she and Laron had seen three days ago were parked on opposite sides of the central square, and Sunay gave that gathering a wide berth, both because of the mob of people around it, and because every single one of her instincts told her to stay away. The outer streets had much less traffic than the central road as well, which made getting to her destination easier.

Navarre Castle's walls would have probably been daunting to the average human, but Sunay wasn't normal. Foxes were surprisingly nimble climbers, and even with the skirt, the foxgirl had little trouble finding the grip she needed to scale the wall and clamber to the top. Her instincts then took over as she dropped down low to survey her surroundings and make sure she remained unseen.

Guards were stationed along the wall near the parapets at equal distances, but their attention was drawn entirely towards either the interior of the palace or out towards the town square. The interior had the other cart from the caravan, and was surrounded by currently unoccupied horses bearing the insignia of the Republican Police.

This... was not good.

Kaeli had told her to run if a situation exactly like this arose, and Sunay deliberately ignored that advice. She needed to find Laron. She needed to know he was okay. She told herself exploring further wouldn't be too dangerous because Laron's room was in the south tower, and all the activity was on the north side.

Climbing *down* a wall would a bit trickier than going up, and the wide open courtyard between the wall and the castle interior was going to be a problem...

Until a hand slapped over her mouth, and a very strong arm

circled around her waist. The foxgirl panicked, and tried to scream until a low voice growled angrily in her ear. “If you want to leave this place alive, you will be silent and follow me.”

Sunay weighed her options, and had come to conclusion to do whatever this man said by the time he actually pulled her through a door leading *inside* the wall. “You're fortunate I recognized you as you approached,” the man said angrily, quietly taking the steps down despite the heavy boots he was wearing. She would have easily thought him one of the guards if it wasn't for the fact that he was behaving very much *not* like them.

“Who... are ya?” Sunay asked. “'Cause you aren't doin' a very good job keepin' people *out* of the castle.”

“I am a guard of the Pontaine family, of which your paramour is a member,” he answered. “As I said, you're lucky I recognized you as the woman Master Laron was with in town three days ago, otherwise I would have had you filled with arrows just for *approaching* the wall.”

“Do *you* have a name?”

The guard shot her a dark glare. “Not one I'm willing to share. Now stop talking before I decide to perform my proper duties rather than extend you the courtesy of one last meeting with your boy.”

One last meeting? It was enough to silence Sunay, since it was clear this “guard” wasn't in any mood to be answering anything further. The man went down another flight of stairs, and turned right, into what was an underground passage that crossed the courtyard.

“These tunnels were designed initially as a way to retreat in case an invader took the wall, but it's also a useful way to move about largely undetected,” he said sternly. “I figured you were about to ask.”

Sunay wasn't actually... and wondered if she should question something so very convenient to her purpose.

The tunnel ended in another set of stairs, this time going up, and ending at the ground floor of the south tower. Sunay was rather surprised to discover that the interior of the castle was as drab and gray as the outside, a red carpet with gold-colored trim and wavy designs covered the primary halls, but outside of that one splash of color, the rest of the castle was dreary gray and iron from the steps to the candelabra on the ceilings... which weren't even lit in lieu of plain torches lining the walls.

“Don't look nervous or curious,” her escort advised. “That will draw attention, which will draw questions.”

Chided, Sunay dropped her head down, and stared intently at her feet.

"And don't look guilty. That will *also* draw suspicion."

Sunay settled for an annoyed snarl, aimed directly at the man in front of her.

"Better. Guards get enough disdain from civilians that no one will bat an eye. Stick with that."

Well, he was making *that* easy enough to manage.

It turned out all the pretenses weren't even necessary, as the pair didn't even pass another guard in their march up to the third floor, much less a member of the Republican Police. Their path came to a stop at a stained oak door directly across the hall from the stairwell. The guard rapped three times, and said, "Laron, you have a visitor. I suggest you make it quick. Republican Police could come for you at any moment."

Sunay immediately stepped forward as the door opened slowly. The Republican Police coming for Laron? Why? Did someone discover his plans to leave?

Laron was confused initially as he stuck his head around the door. "Donovan? I have a visitor?" Then he yelped. "Sunay! You're alright! Thank the Coders!"

He quickly pulled the foxgirl inside his room while Sunay's head swam with bewilderment. *He* was worried about *her?* "What is goin' on Laron? Why are the Republican Police comin' fer ya?"

"There's no time," Laron insisted. "You have to get away from this place as fast as you can. Away from the orphanage, all of Avalon, you aren't safe here."

"Why? What has happened?"

"Cavalier Norman revealed some indiscretions of my father's and my father betrayed the orphanage in order to avoid execution. Norman's mustering a mob to burn down and massacre the whole lot of you."

Sunay's knees trembled, and her face disfigured in terror. She was so petrified by the thought that Laron had to shake her out of her stupor. "I... have to get back to the orphanage and warn them!"

She tried to leave, but Laron held her fast. "No! You can't!"

"Why not?" The foxgirl demanded incredulously.

"I think they're after *you*, Sunay."

"Why in the burnin' pits would they be after *me?*"

There was another rap on the door, and Laron opened it to confirm it was Donovan rather than the police. "There's no time. You *have* to get out of here, any way you can. You can *not* let the Republican Police or anyone in Avalon find you." He dashed to his dresser, and pulled out an envelope. "These are your travel papers. Keep hidden, and get out of this Coders' forsaken land."

"Come with me then!"

Laron shook his head. "My family is already being gathered to be sent to Snake River and the Judges there, where we will be evaluated for our merit to the Republic. If I were to disappear, it would start a manhunt. The very notability that would have made it possible for me to leave without question before makes it impossible for me to leave now."

"Master Laron, I hear footsteps in the damn stairwell. I think it's safe to say it's the Republic," Donovan warned angrily from the other side of the door.

Laron then shoved Sunay out the door, with one last imperative, "Go! Now!" He then shut the door and refused the one plea for answers Sunay was able to voice before Donovan yanked her away.

The guard led her left, rather than back down the stairwell. "We have to go around our Republican friends," he explained. "Don't make any noise, and if I tell you to run, you do so as fast as your legs can carry you."

Sunay heard what Donovan was saying, but with the immediate adrenaline rush faded, she had fallen into a deep worried melancholy.

Donovan tried to reassure her by saying, "Master Laron will be fine. It's his father that's in trouble. In these cases, the family is merely gathered as a matter of procedure to keep them from plotting against Parliamentary action. He's much more concerned for you, even if I don't know why."

He led her into a stairwell on the opposite side of the tower, where Sunay revealed exactly why by yanking off her skirt. If she needed to potentially run fast, that garment was only going to get in the way. "Well, that explains a great deal," Donovan grumbled as he turned to see Sunay's tail twitching nervously.

For a moment, Sunay froze, worried that she had made a terrible mistake revealing her chimera traits too soon, and that the guard would turn on her. Instead, Donovan grumbled, "Should have figured Laron would fall for the first cute girl with a fluffy tail," then spun back about and resumed his path.

"You're... not... upset by it?" Sunay asked.

The guard scoffed. "Never understood why the church would turn their ire on the poor sots born of such sinful acts, rather than the nobles *committing* them. Besides, considering *my* birth was no doubt what prompted Laron's grandmother to curse the fool to begin with, I really wouldn't have much grounds in which to judge."

That explained the familiarity between Laron and the seemingly nondescript guard.

The tunnel they entered was different than the one they entered the castle tower in. Donovan pointed down toward the end of the path, and said, "This will allow you exit to the south side of the castle beyond the castle wall, and away from all the commotion. I'm not sure where you'll need or want to go from there, but at least you'll be mostly out of sight while you go about it."

"Thank ya," Sunay said.

"You're welcome. For what little help I've been." He reached the end of the tunnel, where a time-worn wooden ladder extended upward. "From here, I'm afraid to say you are on your own. Good luck."

Donovan pushed himself against the wall to give Sunay room to pass, and she regarded the ladder warily. She was *not* heavy, and she wasn't even sure that rickety thing would hold her weight. She felt safer digging her fingers into the dirt *behind* the ladder and climbing up that way.

There wasn't much space at the top of the hole, but she could clearly see the way out through the crawl space, emerging out into the open sky after only three meters or so. Looking back, had she not known about the tunnel, she would have thought it to be nothing more than an abandoned animal den. Pretty slick escape route in case of an invasion.

But her mind quickly turned to the east, and the forest in the distance. She had to believe she wasn't too late.

Sunay dropped to all fours, willing every last bit of energy into moving as fast as she could, even as fatigue built up, and her body protested, her mind refused to let herself slow. She *had* to be in time... she couldn't afford to be too slow and a minute too late.

A clue that she wasn't came from the sound of horse hooves to the north, and the grumble of a mob in the distance. While she was at the bottom of a rise, and couldn't see them, she could hear there were a lot of them and that they were still heading east. That gave her the surge of adrenaline she needed for a second wind, charging into the tree line ahead of the mob.

Her route also gave her a more direct path to the orphanage rather than the road, but even then Sunay figured she wouldn't have much time. She more trampled over the forest than through it; weaving through trees, charging through brush, and even spooking a *bear* as she barreled past without regard for her own safety.

Sunay burst into the clearing, which mercifully held a still standing orphanage within, no doubt looking like she had been dragged through a hedge backwards. Considering how she had plowed through a wide rose bush not even a minute before, it would have been fairly close to the truth.

"Matron!" she screamed with surprising force considering how heavily she was panting. "Matron! *Maaaaaaatron!*"

Sunay opened the front door with her head as much as her hand, still bellowing out for Matron Miriam. Not surprisingly, the noise drew the attention of many of the bratlings and Kaeli before Miriam slammed her door open, irritated by the racket.

"*Sunay!* What has gotten into...?"

The foxgirl interrupted the matron's question, grabbing Miriam by the collar of her robe, and saying, "Ya have to get everyone outta here! *Now!*"

Sunay knew her behavior would panic the little ones, but there wasn't time to worry about their sensibilities. Matron Miriam however, didn't have a grasp of the situation yet. "Whatever for? Sunay, you are scaring the children!"

"Laron's dad has ratted us out! There's a mob comin' to burn this whole place down and everyone in it!"

Miriam was aghast. "What? How do you know this?"

"You can yell at me and punish me later! But right now, we need to get everyone outta here!"

Sunay knew she looked crazed, and that there was probably little reason to believe her at first glance, but Matron Miriam was a careful woman and the orphanage hadn't lasted for years by dismissing threats to it. The older woman stared straight into Sunay's eyes for a long, pregnant pause, then shouted, "Kaeli! I need everyone assembled in the back yard for a roll call, and I need it done fast!"

The beargirl had been hovering at the doorway to her kitchen, and immediately jumped to action, saying calmly, "Come along, little ones. You heard the matron. Let's get to the back, don't dally now. Hurry up."

Sunay expected crying and panic from the youngest children, but the bratlings put on the bravest faces they could, doing credit to how Miriam had raised them to be as strong as they needed to be. The matron didn't break eye contact with Sunay even after she started walking away, silently chiding the foxgirl even as she showed intense pain. Miriam didn't need an explanation. She knew how Sunay would have found out what she had. Betrayal was warring with serendipity, and Matron Miriam didn't know how she was going to deal with it yet.

"Help Kaeli and me round up the brood, will you?" the matron finally ordered, her voice level and calm. "Go out into the front yard and tell them about the roll call."

Sunay complied, the latest burst of adrenaline starting to leave her as she relayed Miriam's order to the perplexed orphans outside.

Megan's ears drooped even lower than normal, and said, "It's bad, isn't it, Sunay?"

"'Fraid so, Meggy, which is why we can't waste time. It's okay to be scared, but if ya listen to the matron, and do what she says, it'll be okay."

The doggirl dropped her spade in the dirt that she had been digging around her flowers with. Megan had spent the last year trying to grow lilies, and now was obviously upset that she had to leave it behind. The poor flowers might survive what was coming, but it wasn't likely.

If the orphans survived today, it was going to be with the clothes they had on their backs, and nothing else.

Sunay had finished her task as the sounds of the angry mob she had passed started reached her ears, most notably the angry howls of hunting dogs. She wasn't the only one that heard it either, as several of the other orphans turned their heads towards the approaching noise as well.

They were out of time.

"Go!" Sunay hissed, ushering her fellow orphans towards the back urgently. Even if they all left *now*, they wouldn't have enough distance before the hounds caught their scent and gave chase, especially with such young ones in the group.

Matron Miriam made the same assessment once word of the dogs made it to her ears. "Kaeli, start leading the children along our evacuation plan. I... I will stay here and keep them busy as long as I can. But you must leave now."

*"I think they're after you, Sunay."*

Laron's words rung in Sunay's head upon Miriam's declaration, and the foxgirl interjected, "No. I'll stay. The bratlings need you. You're the only thing keeping them from losing their minds, and they're gonna need you more than ever now."

Miriam would have nothing of it. "Sunay, what do you think you'll..."

"I don't have time to explain, but I can keep a pack of dogs and their hunting mutts busy for a long time, I bet. But y'all gotta get goin', and fast. There's no time to argue. You can yell at me later."

She left out the part where she didn't anticipate there *being* a later.

Sunay didn't give Matron Miriam or anyone else opportunity to interject, dropping down and dashing towards the north, towards the road, and to the approaching mob. The foxgirl figured even if Laron was wrong, that she'd at least get attention by being a chimera.

If he was *right*... then she wouldn't have to worry about why. That was a plus, wasn't it?

Sunay veered slightly off the road to the right and into the brush, slowing down to try and stay out of detection for as long as possible. She wanted to get their attention, but not just yet. She saved that big entrance for once the mob was in sight, and she was able to get a good luck at who she was up against.

Surprisingly, she didn't see a lot of uniformed police; the bulk of the mob was civilian, carrying torches and hunters with bows and straining to hold back their hounds. In the center of that mass of people was a man riding a dappled brown and white horse, dressed in noble finery, a white suit coat and neatly pressed pants with blue stripes that ran down the sides. His hair was mostly gray with flecks of brown, and his face carried the look of a man who had seen a few fights in his days.

That was no doubt who Laron called Cavalier Norman.

The hounds picked up her scent, as the two closest to her started sniffing the air and leaning in her direction. At that point, Sunay needed to move while she still had the element of surprise. It was time to see if the Dog of the Republic could outsmart a fox.

She leaned back then lunged forward, hitting full stride before she even reached the road. Not even the hounds had time to react as Sunay charged through the mob, then tackled Cavalier Norman off his horse, regaining her feet and scampering to the other side of the road before the group could even fully sort out what had happened.

Sunay swished her tail animatedly, making sure it caught Cavalier Norman's attention as he scrambled to his feet, his once immaculate suit now streaked with dirt. He glared with murderous intent as Sunay taunted, "Hey, Dog! Lookin' fer me?"

The Cavalier's eyes bulged, and he pointed directly at the foxgirl while bellowing, "There! That's the one! Thirty silver to the one that brings me her corpse!"

Well, Laron *was* right.

Sunay turned tail and disappeared into the forest, the howls of foxhounds following on her tail. She wasn't very worried about being chased down; hounds weren't particularly fast, and hunted foxes through tenacity and smell rather than speed. She wasn't going to be able to escape, but that wasn't important.

She turned her pursuers to the west, away from the orphans whose evacuation path would take them east. She didn't have a set destination in mind, but she figured the further north and west she went, even if it meant taking her out of the forest, the better the chance the rest of the orphans had to get to something resembling safety.

*South.*

The thought that entered her mind was so out of the blue, and didn't even feel like hers. It rattled her so much that she actually tripped over a partially uncovered tree root, and fell flat on her belly and got a mouthful of damp forest dirt. Going south was *insane*. She wouldn't have far to run before she reached the ocean, and on the beach she'd be easily cornered, if not shot dead.

*You must go South. You have been chosen.*

Okay... now she *knew* these weren't her thoughts. Chosen for what? To die a gruesome death in a shallow sandy grave? But even as she thought how stupid such a move would be, her legs seemed to have gained a will of their own, moving her quickly to the south and the coast. Any attempts to fight that urge or uncertainty only slowed her down, and she quickly stopped fighting it. Whatever was in her head, it seemed the better idea to follow its instructions.

Sunay knew little about the direction she was going in, having only seen it from a distance and through the cover of trees and brush. She knew there was effectively *no* cover for about two miles once the forest broke, only flat grassland with a gentle decline until it turned to sand.

The sand was wet and packed well, but there was still far more give than Sunay liked, and she felt her speed drop sharply the moment her feet started sinking into the surface. It felt similar to trying to run through mud, and it wasn't pleasant.

The hounds were gaining ground as well, though Sunay figured they'd be as slowed by the wet sand as much as she was. The worry was the men *following* the hounds, with their bows that would have no concern for the terrain.

*West. You will find safety there.*

The directions still didn't make any sense. To the west, the ground level started to rise, forming what amounted to a miniature cliff face, and the beach wrapped around it to form a cove. How would that be safe? If anything, it would be her grave site if there wasn't some other access point.

As she took a sharp turn to right, that's when she saw the ships in the distance, one a grand galleon if she remembered her lessons on naval vessels properly, with four huge masts bearing black and gold sails, striped diagonally from upper left to lower right. With it were three smaller frigates with entirely different sail patterns, one a white field with a gold leaf, the second red with a white cross vertical and horizontal, and the third black with a white skull.

Those weren't the colors of the Republic of Avalon, nor were they the colors of Aramathea, which were scarlet and violet by her memory.

They were the colors of pirate ships.

The five men gathered in the cove, around the remains of a campfire, were no doubt members of their crews. Sunay couldn't decide if that was a good or a bad thing, as while pirates would certainly have no love for an Avalonian torch mob, she doubted they'd be welcoming some stranger running up to them torn up from the forest and screaming for her life.

Yet her legs kept moving forward, even as she caught the pirates' attention. She finally stopped, dropping to her elbows, her tail hanging limp and her ears drooped in fatigue. Sunay forced herself to look up as one of the pirate rose from a cross-legged sitting position, and slowly approached with deliberate strides.

Sitting down he had been nearly as tall as his compatriots, and once standing he left no doubt of his stature. Sunay figured this giant of a man was at least nine feet tall, and about as wide, covered from head to toe in scarves and thick clothing, except for two amber eyes with vertically slit pupils. He looked overdressed for a northern *winter*, much less autumn in the Versilles Province.

He lorded over the foxgirl in disquieting silence, his head jerked up upon hearing the howls of the hounds pursuing her. The towering man then moved towards the approaching dogs, Sunay rolling over and pushing herself onto her elbow to see just what in the pits he was thinking.

The first dog turned the bend into the cove at full speed, and got kicked to the jaw for its effort. Sunay cringed as she heard bone crack and flesh tear. The hound took a sickening arc before crashing into the cove wall, where crunching bone registered again and the dog dropped lifelessly to the sand.

The next foxhound pounced, then was intercepted by the back of the shrouded man's left hand. More gruesome sounds followed, and that dog skipped twice across the wet beach before, dead before it even came to a stop. A third used the opening to attack the man's leg, fangs sinking deep as the dog twisted its head back and forth to try and take down its victim.

Instead, the giant man shook the dog off with an effortless flick of his shin, and with quickness that someone his size should not have possessed brought that same leg down on the hound's head, crushing its skull in one continuous motion.

Sunay was dumbstruck, and wouldn't have been able to say anything more than incoherent babbling even if she'd had the strength to speak. His companions had stepped forward in the meantime, helping the foxgirl to her feet, bemusedly noting her astonishment. "Eh, da Admiral there is goin' easy on 'em so far. Just wait until you see 'im git serious," said the first one, a short, somewhat plump, half bald man in a red and white striped shirt and black pants.

Another, a taller lankier fellow, with a furred face like a badger said, "Lookin' like that's gonna be about now."

The remaining dogs had fallen back, instead holding position at the edge of the cove, barking angrily, while their human support finally caught up. Seeing the already dead dogs, one of the mob let an arrow loose, thudding with fatal accuracy into the Admiral's chest.

Or... *should* have been fatal accuracy. The massive pirate regarded the shot in the same way Sunay regarded a thorn in her clothing. Distastefully, he pulled the offending weapon out, snapped it in half, then pounced.

The giant covered the fifty feet between him and his attacker in one bound, tackling the bowman, then grabbing him by the neck and throwing him like he was a rag doll into the mob. From there, the

Admiral drew a black steel serrated tulwar from his belt, and cleaved another of the mob clean through, from shoulder to hip, in one stroke.

That effectively got the mob's attention, and the civilians among the gang broke with fear, stumbling over themselves and knocking Cavalier Norman from his horse again as they fled. The Republican Police units held their ground, but their knees betrayed that the fact that it wouldn't take much to send them running like frightened children.

As he pushed himself up to his feet again, Norman bellowed, "Cowards! Return this instant! It's *one man!*"

That "one man" then tossed aside two of the police effortlessly, ignored the slash of a third, and grabbed the cavalier by the neck, and lifting the officer smoothly off the ground. At that point, even the Republican Police broke ranks, only occasionally sparing concern towards the cavalier in the pirate's death grip.

The pirate admiral finally spoke, a deep guttural growl that made Sunay cringe, and she wasn't even the target of his ire. "This woman is under my protection from this point forward," he said. "Any further attack on her is an attack on my crew."

He then threw Norman down under the cavalier's horse. "Now be gone. You will not receive another warning."

Either out of pride or stupidity, Norman sputtered, "I'll return with an army if I have to!"

"We won't be here, so it would be a waste of your time and your manpower. But if that will make you feel you accomplished something, you are welcome to do so."

The giant man turned about, no longer giving even the slightest concern to the Republican officer, who climbed back onto his horse and beckoned the animal into a gallop.

"I think dat fellow learned 'is lesson," the short pirate smirked. "Ya don't mess wit' da Admiral."

Said admiral had returned to his crew, stopping directly in front of Sunay. He probably didn't intend to violate her personal space, but Sunay discovered her bubble of personal space expanded depending on how large the other person was. She gulped, twitched her fingers in a nervous wave, and said, "Hiya. I'm... Sunay. Th... thank you... maybe?"

"I am Ahmin, I am the Admiral of the Gold Pirates," he said sternly, but without the snarl he had addressed Cavalier Norman with. "The men with you are Captain Roberts," gesturing to the short pirate, "Captain Drake," to the badger faced man, "Captain Jones," to the currently silent man in red, "and Captain Davey," to the man in blue.

"A... pleasure to meet ya... all of ya."

Admiral Ahmin said simply, "You have been chosen to join my crew."

Her dander rose with such a declarative statement. "And I don't get a say in the matter?"

"To those who have been chosen, there is no choice." He stated it as factually as if he was telling her the weather. "Your calling is with us. Though for what it is worth, I think you'd find us a much more preferable option to being alone in a land that quite actively wants you dead."

Sunay had to admit that was a compelling point.

"You will serve directly under me on my vessel, the *Goldbeard*."

Sunay nodded timidly.

"Are you ready to go?" Ahmin asked sternly. "We really don't have time to dawdle."

Sunay then became quite concerned about the orphanage. "Hey... there were other chimeras... like me. They fled southeast. There was a plan to evacuate... but I don't know..."

Ahmin looked over Sunay's shoulder. "Roberts. Find out which handlers on the Line will be responsible for Miriam and her charges. Impress upon them that any harm, any at all, that comes to any of those young and old, will be as harm to my crew."

Roberts bowed. "Aye aye, Admiral."

Sunay's head whipped back and forth between the two pirates. "Waita minute... ya know the matron?"

"I know much about you and the people around you, Sunay. After all, you have been chosen."

The foxgirl had to ask, because it was evident the admiral wasn't talking merely about being a pirate. "Chosen... for what? By who?"

The cloth around Ahmin's face shifted upwards. The brigand was smiling. "If you earn my trust, you will learn. Now are there any other pressing issues or questions? Because I do wish to set sail quickly before our Cavalier friend finds more men to throw at us."

Sunay looked back to the north. Perhaps Matron Miriam and the orphans were safe, if she took Admiral Ahmin at his word, but she didn't know if Laron was going to be all right, or even if he would be released by the Republic, though if Cavalier Norman represented the typical Republican supporter, she doubted it.

Thoughts of the young man reminded her of the gift he had given her, still tucked away in the pocket of her trousers, still in its red velvet box. She removed the earring, dropped the box to the sand, then clipped the piece of jewelry into one of the piercings in her right ear. That would be her promise... to one day come back and find out what happened to everyone she cared about, and grieve if need be.

Sunay then turned to her new crew, and said with a sharp nod, “Yeah. Let's go.”

# Chapter Five: You Are a Pirate

Sunay had heard more than a few things about life on a pirate ship before she actually served on one, from filthy conditions, violence, and the cutthroat nature that came from living on whatever you could pillage or kill.

The *Goldbeard* did not reflect those things, though Sunay wasn't sure if that meant the stories were wrong or if Admiral Ahmin's craft and crew were the exception. The ship was expertly maintained with the finest lumber, the sails frequently replaced with whole cloth, weapons periodically cleaned and sharpened, and even the decks mopped to a shine regularly.

Sunay knew this because she was frequently assigned to that last part over the last three months, though Ahmin *had* called a stop to that chore as fall was steadily turning to winter and they were sailing to the northern provinces of Avalon.

The labor didn't bother her, she was used to cleaning, and had told Ahmin so when Jacques, his first mate, first shoved the mop into her hand. He also assigned her spot repairs when she demonstrated she could learn how to do so quickly. Honestly, being comfortable with the harness they dangled her from was the hardest part of the whole thing.

"Ah, I'm sure that there's a lot of truth about pirates in the stories that are told. But I would not be privy to such squalor, which should tell you all you need to know that the tales need not apply to this ship and this crew. The Gold Pirates have resources as strong as any navy on the whole of the continent, don't ever doubt that."

She looked up, towards the first platform on the main sail, where Joffe was reclining in a canvas sling that he had attached to the platform using some twine, sipping coconut milk straight from the coconut itself, answering the thought she had just aired.

Joffe was *certainly* not one that would fit the pirate idiom; he was an educated man, and didn't pretend otherwise. He was well traveled and well learned, born in Caravel, was taught philosophy in Aramathea, and how to make black powder from masters of the craft outside of Reaht, knowledge nearly lost to the Void when the eastern continent of Xanadu collapsed nearly thirty years ago.

He always dressed neatly, though also practically; his canvas trousers and thick cotton shirt with a leather vest and small bow tie were a staple outfit of his, yet he would roll up his sleeves if dirty work was needed. And it frequently was, as his clothes would become streaked with oil that needed prompt cleaning before it stained permanently.

She knew that because she often did laundry as well.

"So why *are* ya here anyway? Other than for makin' candles?"

Candles were the term Ahmin coined to refer to the small rockets that the *Goldbeard* and other ships in the Gold Pirate fleet used to communicate with each other, with different colors and burst patterns to signal anything from their presence, to calling for another ship for aid, to even launching a coordinated attack on a target.

"And is that not enough?" he replied indignantly. "Why, I could make a rocket that could propel a ship if I wanted to!"

"Yes, and probably set half the ship on fire while yer at it."

Juno was a "natural" chimera, the result of a pagan ritual in lands north of what was now Reaht, proving devotion to a "spider god", which was the reason for her six blood red eyes arranged laterally across her face, short bristly gray and brown ticked hair, and a pair of three inch long fangs that protruded from her upper lip.

But despite that fearsome visage, Juno was the gentlest little thing Sunay had ever met... as long as you weren't a fly. Juno would definitely hurt a fly. And a mosquito. And any other flying insect that got a little too close to the ship at night. And rodents. And occasionally birds. And possibly a sparklebunny, though that was just hearsay.

So maybe Juno *wasn't* the gentlest little thing Sunay had ever met. But close.

That heritage also allowed her to have a spider's "stickiness", the girl was able to climb up and down nearly any surface effortlessly, like the masts, which was why her primary responsibility was the rigging and the sails, from which she had just descended face first directly above Joffe's head. The engineer yelped in surprise, tumbling out of his hammock and falling on his left side onto the deck with a thump.

"Every... damn... time..." Joffe grumbled. "You'd think I'd be used to it by now..."

"You'd think so!" the spidergirl agreed, spinning around the mast to avoid Joffe's cot and then landing on the deck with a half flip to right herself. "Got the replacement rope up on the sails, Jacques! The rowin' team can take a break!"

Jacques was the one responsible for managing much of the day-to-day goings on of the ship while the admiral handled the large scale planning and coordination of both this ship and all the others in the fleet.

He was a bit of an enigma, as unlike the rest of the crew he didn't freely talk about himself. He wasn't unfriendly or distant, just that he claimed his life was fairly "boring." But as Matron Miriam had liked to say, "a man with gray has seen many things," and Jacques definitely had many a silver thread in his mane of otherwise dark blonde hair.

"I'll pass the word along," Jacques said, "Go on and lower the sails, Juno. Bolin, keep us on course!"

Bolin was the primary helmsman for the *Goldbeard*, having nearly a decade of experience sailing large vessels like the galleon he was currently steering. He didn't terribly look the part of a helmsman, being thin and wiry, but his frame betrayed finely toned arm muscles that, combined with his experience, could handle the *Goldbeard* with a precision that Sunay would not have thought possible for a ship so large.

His identical twin, Balco, manned the crow's nest. Balco kept his blonde hair long which was rather handy for a couple reasons: first, it allowed for easy identification between him and his short haired brother, and secondly was as good of an indicator that he was in the nest as the red flag at the top of the wooden bucket that was effectively his station.

"Winter's Cape! Comin' up ahead! 77 degrees and five miles!"

Jacques took that announcement and relayed it to Bolin even though that probably wasn't necessary. Then he turned to Sunay, and ordered, "Sunay, go down to the admiral's cabin and let him know we are on our approach. Inform him I have the supply manifest ready and just need him to sign off on it."

The foxgirl gulped nervously, but nonetheless made her move to the stairwell at the fore side of the boat towards the lower decks. The interior of the *Goldbeard* was dark, and it took Sunay a moment for her eyes to adjust from the shift in light. Some pirates claimed wearing a patch over one eye helped the transition, but the crew of the *Goldbeard* by and large didn't find the practice worth it, especially since it had a tendency to mess with depth perception.

Once she felt confident that her eyesight had adjusted, she slowly navigated the stairway. The lower levels were as tidy and well maintained as the deck itself, with furs rolled up along the walls in anticipation of the coming winter, when they would pinned to the walls to try and provide insulation. Sunay was dubious about how effective that would be, but at the same time guessed little was better than none.

Admiral Ahmin's cabin was on the third deck, at the fore end after all the cots for the rest of the crew, and she took that walk across the length of the ship with terrified steps. To be fair, she knew her fear was completely irrational. If Admiral Ahmin didn't think she had a use, or just didn't like her for whatever reason, she would not be on board.

But rationality wasn't always a comfort when that massive slab of chimeric humanity was staring you down with an impassive stare.

Sunay knew he was a chimera. His eyes were slitted, more like those of a cat than a human, though what *type* of chimera and what animal was influenced on him was a mystery. A mystery he seemed intent on keeping, as the only person who seemed to have *any* idea about the details was Jacques, and the first mate was keeping mum on that score intentionally.

The admiral's cabin door wasn't any different than any other door on the ship, except for the fact that it was his. It was always closed, and surrounded by an aura that said, "Keep Out." But it was an aura she had to ignore. Jacques ordered her to do this. The admiral wouldn't kill her for *that*.

She wanted to slap herself when her fist hesitated at the door. Then she followed it up by barely tapping her knuckles against the wood. She grumbled to herself, and addressed the door for another attempt when said door flew inward and the admiral stood in the now open doorway glaring down at her.

"What is it?"

He could have been grumpy. Or not. Sunay's ears still hadn't caught the difference, if there even was any.

"The first mate wanted me to tell ya that we're almost to Winter's Cape."

"Good."

"And that he has the manifest ready and just needs you sign off on it."

"I'll do that when we drop anchor," the admiral answered. "Anything else?"

"N... no, sir."

There was silence for a moment, and Sunay hovered nervously. She knew by now that she had not been dismissed and thus shouldn't leave, but didn't want to speak up and potentially upset the admiral for interrupting his thoughts. Fortunately, he spoke up before she had to.

"Let Jacques know that the crew can be dismissed for three hours," the admiral ordered. "Stretch your legs, take it easy. I'll handle the resupply and watch the ship. Dismissed."

Sunay wasn't about to argue those orders, both because they were a welcome surprise and that she *really* didn't want to second guess the admiral. She spun about and made a full retreat as the admiral slammed his door shut, then dropped to all fours as she scrambled up the steps to the deck. The foxgirl was moving so fast she forgot to stop and let her eyes adjust when she emerged outside, momentarily blinded by the abrupt increase in light.

Staggering, she bumped straight into Jacques, who only responded with an amused laugh at the foxgirl's antics. Sunay shot a squinted glare in what she thought was his direction while blinking repeatedly, then relayed the admiral's orders to a chorus of hearty cheers.

"Juno!" the first mate hollered. "Help Sunay ready the boats! We're gonna need the lot of them!"

The spidergirl dropped down to the deck, grabbing Sunay by the arm and leading her to the railing where the rowboats were tied to the side of the hull. Each one had to be untied from the brackets that held them, then rigged to the winch that would lower them down to the water level. It was not an easy process, especially if you needed to prepare several, so the extra hands were useful.

"Hey, greenhorn," Juno said, grabbing Sunay's attention as she was tying a hitch into a metal loop on the rowboat in front of her. "Yer comin' with me and the rest of the crew, got it?"

The foxgirl blinked. Usually the crew went their own separate ways when given shore leave. Granted, Sunay rarely did more than wander around and worry about all those she left behind, but she doubted she'd be terribly good company anyway. "The rest of the crew?"

"This isn't really shore leave," Juno explained. "A supply run rarely takes more than a few hours. Jacques hands the manifest over to the harbor master, and the shipping company in charge loads 'er up. Sometimes the admiral gives us all a break like this. So we all go crash at the nearest pub or tavern, have a couple drinks, and relax."

"I'm too young to drink by Avalonian law," Sunay noted.

"Yer not allowed to be a chimera by Avalonian law, either,"

Juno said. "Yer technically a mercenary sailor, not beholden to any city or country. Besides, the law is that yer not allowed to be found *drunk* before a certain age. You'll be fine. We can't get roarin' drunk or anythin' since we aren't stayin' in town anyway. It'll be a good time. Yer comin', and you don't have the option."

Sunay sighed, relenting to what she knew was a lost battle. "Fine, but don't expect me to lead any drinkin' songs."

"Nah, the only halfways decent signer on this ship is Gurgn, and he only knows Reahtan battle hymns. Not really good celebration material there."

That got Sunay to giggle, which even she admitted was a pretty rare occurrence along with cracking a smile or being anything like how she used to be. "Alright, ya win. I take it ya know this place, then?"

"Jacques better than the rest of us, but yeah, we've supplied here a few times. Kinda tucked away and hard to reach for most of the Republic, so it makes for a good place for those who would like to stay out of the eyes of Caravel and the Parliament."

Jacques stepped in to help them with the last boat. "Which also means it can get a bit rough," he said, "and as such, we want to stick together as a group. If trouble wants to find us that badly, it's best to face it all as one."

Sunay understood the wisdom in that. Perhaps she could find a corner to slink into quietly and not interrupt anyone else's fun.

"Winter's Cape! One mile!" Balco shouted.

"I don't want to get much closer," Bolin informed. "There's a shelf comin' up quick, very uneven and rises sharply."

Jacques shouted down to the lower decks. "Gurgn! Drop anchor! Juno, raise the sails!"

The spidergirl dashed to the main mast, disappearing into the rigging, as the deck trembled slightly and the metallic clatter of the heavy iron anchor and the chain it was attached to dropped towards the sea floor.

Seconds later, the black and gold striped main sail swiftly rose in opposition to Juno's sliding down the mast with a rope between her teeth. She tied it down and locked the sails in position before making an effortless leap to another mast to repeat the process... all without even touching the deck.

"I don't think I'll ever stop being amazed watching Juno work," Sunay remarked.

Jacques shook his head. "Greenhorn, I remember days when it

could take five strapping lads to manage the sails. What you're seeing is Joffe's skill more than Juno's."

The scholar scoffed. "Mere child's play, really. Simple machines that maximize application of work. Any novice engineer could whip up a few pulleys and rig them together."

The first mate laughed softly. "Devising a system that does the work of five men? Child's play. Making a candle burn purple instead of orange? *That's* the problem of the ages."

"It requires a special kind of salt, I am sure," Joffe grumbled. "Sylvite comes close... I think I just need one more ingredient."

Ahmin then appeared from below decks, straightening once he cleared the doorway. He said nothing as he crossed the deck, stopped in front of Jacques who pulled out a rolled up sheet of parchment, took said parchment, looked it over, signed it, handed it back to Jacques, and retreated to the main mast, where he leaned back with his arms crossed and his eyes closed.

Sunay's ears flattened nervously. He looked unhappy, but Jacques and Juno did not share that concern. "I sometimes think he sends us all off because it's the only time he can get a good bit of shut eye and not be cooped up in his cabin," the spider girl whispered.

"Alright people, fall in!" Jacques bellowed as the crew congregated. Juno grabbed Sunay and pushed the foxgirl into formation next to her.

That had hardly been the first time Juno had done such, but even now Sunay wondered if that was normal for the "greenhorn", the term the crew used to describe the newest or most inexperienced member. She didn't dare ask, and appear even more novice than she already was.

Jacques issued their parting orders, saying, "I wish to reiterate this is *not* shore leave. It is a supply break. We will stay together, and we will return together. If you are left behind, consider your conscription aboard this ship void. I trust there is no confusion."

Sunay echoed the rest of the crew in confirmation, and Jacques continued. "We will disembark following standard protocol. You all know your normal ship numbers, and you will keep them, with these exceptions: Second shift crew will take the five boats on the port side aft. Third shift crew will take the boats on the starboard side. First shift crew take their normal boat assignments. Juno, lower the second shift. Sunay, lower the third. You two then join me on my boat. We will all assemble again once we're on shore. Dismissed!"

Lowering the boats was easier than prepping them and a lot

easier than raising them. Once they were tied, they were effectively free floating, which meant she could push them away from the railing even with them full, and the "passive resistance" of the pulley, as Joffe called it, allowed for the weight of the boat and occupants to lower itself. About the only thing Sunay had to do was make sure the mechanism didn't break, which was apparently possible though "highly unlikely with proper maintenance."

With her boats away, Sunay moved back to the port side, and the first boat with Jacques, Juno, and Joffe. Once they were settled in, Ahmin himself lowered the final boat, and Jacques took the oars to propel them the remaining distance.

Winter's Cape wasn't named such because it was a particularly arctic climate, though like most of Northern Avalon it definitely *could* get cold and snowy. As Sunay understood it, the name came from the founder being named "Winter." She hoped to the Coders that was his surname.

It wasn't even all that much of a cape, either... a low lying hill that maybe was fifty feet over sea level at its crest and jutted a quarter mile out past the rest of the coast. The town itself didn't even rest on the part that was actually the cape, instead the docks were on the coastline to the south, and the town a good half mile inland.

The Harbormaster of Winter's Cape was a seedy-looking sort, hunched over and using a cane to help with his balance, heavily scarred face and hands, and an eye patch that was quite possibly covering up a missing eye. He shambled to meet Jacques, who had pushed his way to the front of the assembly, and handed over the manifest. "The galleon off that way. Black and gold sails. Hard to miss it."

The Harbormaster nodded and handed off the manifest to his second, a younger and more healthy boy around Sunay's age. "Get the men to load up the barge, boy. I trust you can handle that now." He then said to Jacques, "I know the *Goldbeard.* So does Goldbeard, and I should warn you he and his crew are in town. Currently makin' a mess of the Main Street Tavern."

The first mate rolled his eyes, and muttered, "Wonderful."

Juno understood at least. Which was good because Sunay was clueless. "Do we go back?" the spidergirl asked.

Jacques scoffed. "No. We have nothing to fear from that wastrel. Him *or* whatever crew of brigands he's assembled. We'll go to Nathan's Tavern. If Goldbeard wants to pick a fight, let him. Let's go, people! Time's a wastin'!"

Sunay highly doubted that the names of the man and the ship

were a coincidence. "Who's this Goldbeard fella?" she asked Juno.

"Daynish raider, Holth Goldbeard is the full name. Not the nicest chap, if you know what I mean. Sorta guy who never thought the Daynish Campaigns really were over. Commandeered a galleon from the Avalonian Navy and used it to raid the coast about fifteen years ago."

"The ship we're using now," Sunay deduced.

"Got it in one," Juno said. "Around that time, the admiral had just become... well... the admiral, and decided that the *Goldbeard* was too good of a ship for Holth. Now, Holth didn't know who the Gold Pirates were, and figured he was dealing with some fledgling pirates with delusions of grandeur. So he challenged the admiral to a Daynish scrum, the winner getting the other's ship. I wasn't there, mind, but I can only imagine the look on Holth's face when he saw that beast appear in front of him.

A Daynish scrum is pretty much how it sounds, it's like a duel without silly things like rules or gentlemanly agreements, and I'm told ol' Holth threw out every trick in the book he could muster, but ya know the admiral's been around and about no few times. Yer not gonna take him by surprise very easily. He kicked Holth's tail pretty soundly, I'm told, to the point that even Holth's crew turned their backs in shame. Kinda surprised that he's still around after that humiliation."

Juno concluded the tale, saying, "Anyway, Avalon was so happy to have Holth's little reign of terror over that they gifted the admiral with the *Goldbeard* and called it even."

Sunay was naturally skeptical, and her eyebrows dropped as her eyes narrowed. "Why do I doubt that last part very much?"

Juno flippantly answered, "'Cause it's a lie. It just sounds like a good ending to the story. Truth is the admiral kept the ship, and Avalon didn't care enough to hunt him down, just like they didn't care too much that Holth had it. The Parliament had, and has, bigger issues."

Sunay could hear the ruckus from the tavern the Harbormaster had mentioned before they even entered the town square. It made the foxgirl wonder why this guy wasn't worth the Parliament's attention, but some foxgirl in an orphanage tucked away in a forest needed a damned army.

Jacques led the crew around the exterior of the square, and laying out details as he did so. "Nathan's isn't as large an establishment, and it's a much nicer place. I don't expect any rowdiness. We're better than the scum in the square, got it?"

"Aye aye, sir!" the crew echoed.

Nathan's lived up to the word of the first mate. It was indeed a fine establishment, red carpet, stained maple tables and chairs with velvet covers. The bar was immaculate, with a white cloth draped across the top. The bartender cringed as the *Goldbeard's* crew filtered in, and the few patrons started to stand nervously to evacuate.

Jacques took the lead, and held up one hand in peace. "At ease, good people, we aren't here to cause or imply any trouble. Is Roland still the owner of this establishment?"

Juno's eyebrows rose as an older half bald man emerged from the floor above, his jaw dropping at the sight of the first mate. Jacques jumped the counter and met the man halfway down, the pair sharing a quiet, if emotionally charged, exchange before he vaulted back over the bar and declared, "Have a seat, everyone. Let's not dally."

"Greenhorn!" Juno declared, grabbing Sunay by the shoulder and not giving the foxgirl much option but to follow her to the table where Bolin and Balco had already taken seats. Jacques followed a moment later, carefully managing five small mugs of what Sunay guessed was lager judging from the deep amber color and large foamy heads. Maybe.

"So... what was *that* about?" Juno queried of the first mate as he slid into the remaining chair. "How do you know that person?"

Jacques replied simply, "A relative."

"So... you're from around here?" she pressed further.

"My extended family is. I was raised in the Free Provinces."

"Why'd your family leave?"

"You'd have to ask them."

This question and answer period matched what she knew of Jacques. He didn't talk about himself much.

Juno then turned to Sunay and said, "See? *This* is why I want you to open up. We already *have* one of you."

Sunay sighed dejectedly. She really *had* been a wet blanket since she came on board, and really didn't offer to many reasons why. "I just didn't wanna depress any of you with things that no one can do anything about."

Juno draped a comforting arm over Sunay's shoulder. "Aww... come on. You're a chimera from Avalon. We kinda already figure whatever it is that it probably is rough. We can take it."

So Sunay told them. About the orphanage, the conditions, the attempt to flee from Cavalier Norman... though leaving out the more personal details, like Laron and the relationship they had. Not even *she* wanted to think too much about that yet.

Juno's jaw went slack, her eyes glistening. “That's... terrible,” she whimpered. “H... how sad... I'm... I'm sorry... And I thought *I* had it rough.”

Jacques gave the spidergirl a cold stare. “Don't be patronizing.”

“I'm not!” Juno protested. “That's awful an' terrible an' sad! No one should have to live a life like that!”

“Because it's so much better to be raised as the manifestation of a god of malice and murder?”

Juno winced, and said meekly, “Oh. *That*.”

“And what is *that* about?” Sunay asked accusingly.

“Nothin',” Juno answered.

Sunay wasn't about to let the spidergirl off that easily. “Oh no, you made me spill, now *you* get to share!”

Juno relented, and said, “It's only fair, I guess. These folks already know the tale, and I guess I never thought to tell you. Ya know the part that I was born from a ritual with some sorta spider spirit, but what I *didn't* say was that I was supposed to be the avatar of that spider god, and I was supposed to rain death and destruction on the approaching Reahtan empire. I guess they didn't realize that I was going to be a kid and not some fully grown force of death.

“I was hidden away in a cave by the Cult of the Great Spider until I was ten, where they tried to train me in being the killer they envisioned. The admiral and his crew found me just before the Reahtan

Jacques chuckled. “The crew of the *Goldbeard* wasn't exactly suited to raise a child. But Juno really didn't have anywhere else to go, and the Admiral feared she was too dangerous to be left with the rest of society. What with the bite that carries a deadly venom and all.”

Juno smiled to show off those fangs. “Can paralyze and kill a bull in twenty seconds. People less.”

“And so you've lived on the *Goldbeard* ever since?” Sunay asked, trying very hard not to think about Juno's teeth and how close they were to the foxgirl's shoulder.

Juno nodded. “Pretty much. Beats livin' in a cave. And don't worry, I only generate venom when I want to. I'm not gonna be killin' anybody by accident.”

Sunay smiled weakly. “Ya know, that isn't as comforting as ya probably think it is.” Desperate to change the topic away from the spider god avatar of murder, she turned her attention to Bolin and Balco. “Please tell me you two have happier backstories.”

The twins gave each other a glance, and Balco spoke up. "As normal as one can expect, I figure," he said. "Our father didn't exactly spare the rod, but we weren't hunted by armies or nothin'. Just yer typical story of 'get so pissed off about your abusive da that you run off to be sailors' story."

"And wind up serving under a massive tower of a man who could flay the skin off your bones with a look," Bolin added. "We didn't start off on the *Goldbeard*, of course. We just did shippin' routes for Grace Shipping Company. Then the Gibraltar Islands became popular, and they started shipping... other cargo."

"He's talking about people," Balco explained. "The Gibraltar islands became a boom town for gold prospectors and adventurers seeking remains of old empires and their lost wealth buried deep within the volcanoes. Now the latter group went willingly, but it *might* surprise you that day to day laborers weren't too keen on living on still-active volcanic islands. So... they were forced to."

"Slaves," Sunay put simply. She didn't need the truth sugarcoated.

"Slaves... indentured servants... whatever you want to call it. All three major empires did it, sometimes seizing the poor, sometimes kidnapping people from nearby Free Provinces. The Grace Shipping Company was one of the worst, by the end of the gold rush, the slave trade was pretty much all Grace did. Bolin and I were told to either get with the new policy or we'd be in the hold rather than on the deck."

Bolin wrapped up the tale. "That's how we found our way into the Gold Pirates. We were approached with helping them break Grace Shipping's trade, and both my brother and I were all for that. By the time Grace got wise to our conveniently sailing repeatedly into pirate raids, we retired from the shipping business, and joined up on the *Goldbeard*."

"So much for happy tales." Sunay sighed. "Now I feel *really* awful about bein' such a louse."

"Oh come now," Juno said. "There's no keepin' score when it comes to tough tales. Besides, none o' us would even be here if we all came from well-adjusted backgrounds. Yer okay, greenhorn. Yer okay."

Jacques also offered assurance. "The Admiral isn't one to bury bad news. If he had learned something, and it wasn't good, he'd tell you. That he hasn't said anything yet means there's hope."

Sunay could either be comforted by her crewmates, or dismiss them. Neither actually changed anything, but one at least made it easier to face any given day. "Thanks, all of ya. I guess... it'll be okay, one way or another, huh?"

*"Hey! I hear you miserable Gold Pirates are in there! Why don't you send out that cheating snake Ahmin and no else needs to get hurt!"*

Jacques cursed under his breath, then muttered more audibly, "Looks like someone ratted us out." He stood, and waved off concern from Roland and the bartender. "I'll handle this, make sure no one leaves until I give them the clear. Crew, follow me."

The *Goldbeard's* crew filed out of the tavern two by two, forming three lines to face their challengers just outside the tavern door. As Jacques had said earlier, they likely weren't going to pose much threat, if for no reason than they were outnumbered forty to six. And they knew it too, Sunay's ears catching whispering amongst amongst themselves of the damn fool thinking he was going to fight the *Goldbeard's* crew. If it came to a fight, those men would look after their own skins first.

While they all certainly lived up to the brigand stereotype, the man who led them did not... nor did he look nearly old enough to have been scrapping with the admiral over a decade ago. His hair and braided beard were a vibrant yellow, his chest, half bare due to the open jerkin over his shoulders, looked vital and strong, glistening from what she guessed was oil. He stood straight and tall, true to the Daynish stereotype. This was a young man, not an old raider.

"Admiral Ahmin isn't here," Jacques said. "He's still on his boat."

"You mean, *my* boat," the Dayne bellowed. "That cheating bastard stole it from my father."

Jacques was not impressed by the claim. "By that line of thinking, the boat still belongs to the Avalonian Navy that your father stole it from. Holth is your father then, boy?"

"Horal, son of Holth, son of Galdberd, Goldbeard by your mangling tongue," the Dayne declared proudly. "And your snake of an admiral should know me well!"

Sunay wasn't sure when or how the admiral appeared, but the massive chimera certainly did, right behind the line of buccaneers assembled behind Horal. "Oh, I do."

The admiral's deep voice panicked all five of Horal's men, and the initially scattered before forming a loose circle around him. The chimera was not at all impressed, not even acknowledging their presence as his eyes, narrowed to slits, bored into the young Dayne that couldn't even match him eye to eye. "I remember you quite well, boy. You're fortunate that your interference got your father to stand down in our scrum, because I would have killed him otherwise."

"You killed him just as dead," Horal accused. "You think he could face his people after being forced to surrender? His hands had to cut his own throat. You didn't defeat him, you humiliated him. And now it's *my* honor on the line. I have to avenge him, and take back what is h..."

The admiral didn't let Horal finish the sentence, sweeping out the Dayne's legs then dropping the young man with a shoulder blow. Horal fell onto his back, then was pinned to the ground by the pirate's boot on the side of his face.

The towering chimera growled, "The *Goldbeard* is not yours. It was *never* yours. It is mine, and you have no claim to it. I will *not* scrum with you, boy. Not now, not a year from now, not a decade from now. Now you take your pet weasels and slink back to whatever dinghy you have stolen for yourself, and leave."

Only then, did he step off of Horal, and let the young Dayne regain his feet. His "weasels" had already fled, and he clearly wasn't going to get the fight he wanted. "This isn't over," he snarled bitterly, even as he fled petulantly.

"Of course it isn't," the admiral grumbled quietly to Horal's retreating back, then exhaled as if it would expel his irritation. "I hope that fool didn't disrupt your kin, Jacques."

Jacques shook his head. "No, sir. He blustered outside and didn't even set one foot in."

"Good. Go back in, pay the bill, and leave them a little extra. Once that's over with I'll meet you back on the ship. The harbormaster's crew did their work in good time. Makes no sense to dally, especially since we've been 'invited' to Tortuga."

Even Sunay knew about that place. The keep of Avalon's most powerful mage, Morgana, and the last official bastion of noble power in the entire country.

"Invited? By the Domina?" Jacques asked.

"Yes," the admiral replied simply.

"Why for?"

"Who knows?" the large pirate said grumpily. "But regardless of the reasons, it's for good relations to pay our respects. So let's march, people. Let's not waste time."

# Chapter Six: The Ice Palace of Tortuga

"Ahoy! Comin' up on Tortuga! 92 degrees and four miles!"

Sunay's head turned further up, towards the crow's nest where the lookout, Balco had bellowed his announcement through the horn that ran from that high location down the mast and flared out towards the helm.

They supplied normally at certain ports all along the western coast of Avalon without harassment, another detail that was far different than what she had been told of pirates. There hadn't been any open sea battles. They hadn't boarded any ships or taken plunder. They didn't need to.

Bolin turned the large wheel while rowing crews in the lower decks helped fight the current. "Can I get a depth, Juno?"

The spidergirl tossed a length of rope with a stone tied to the end over the railing, then once it hit the bottom found the water depth. "Got about fifty feet, Bolin!"

Large vessels, like the *Goldbeard*, rested far too low in the water to approach most docks safely, and the docks connected to Tortuga were clearly among that number. Fifty feet was *not* much clearance considering ten feet of the craft was below water and that the sea floor was hardly even, with outcrops, ridges, coral, and other formations that could easily rip through a wooden hull.

"This'll have to be close enough. Even if the water was deep, I don't like the ice as we get closer," Bolin said, even as he gazed out into the distance. Tortuga was not close at all... at least another four miles away. It was going to be a *long* row to shore.

Ahmin emerged from below decks, straightening with a sigh of relief once he was out in the open. Bolin immediately relayed the news. "I donna want to get any closer, Admiral. The water's low already."

"It will be fine, Bolin," the towering pirate replied. "We won't be supplying, so there won't be any hard rowing in store. Sunay, you're with me."

The foxgirl's eyes bulged. Her? Whatever for?

"No one else?" Jacques asked as he approached from the bow of the ship.

"No. Just Sunay and me. No time for shore leave either. I do not anticipate a long visit."

The crew on the deck all started looking at each other knowingly, and Sunay did not like it one bit. "What is goin' on here? Why are you all lookin' like that?"

Ahmin interrupted, shouting gruffly, "Sunay! To me. *Now.*"

Sunay gulped, her mind racing over what she could have possibly done to earn the Admiral's ire. Everything she had done had met his approval... unless... could he have been disappointed about her attempted patch job in the cooking hold two weeks ago? But that didn't make sense... he even said it was a decent enough job for the first time she had ever worked with pitch... and it had been properly fixed within two days after they had dropped anchor at Canary Island.

What else could she have done? She took pride in her work, and did not sense that she had upset any of the other crew. Ahmin demanded respect on his ship, and she felt she followed that to the letter, going out of her way to *not* start trouble either on or off the ship.

"Sunay!"

The admiral's order startled her into compliance, the foxgirl shuffling swiftly towards the giant pirate while trying to ignore the chuckles from the rest of the crew. Ahmin pointed to the rowboat, silently ordering to climb in. Sunay lifted her legs over the deck railing one at a time, sitting down on the fore bench and looking forward towards Tortuga.

Admiral Ahmin followed, taking a seat on the aft end, and ordered that the boat be lowered to the water level. A crank and pulley system did the work, and Joffe's expert maintenance made the twenty foot descent smooth with almost no jostling.

The Admiral himself took to the oars, his powerful strokes cutting through the calm waters swiftly. Sunay kept her eyes and ears forward at the rapidly approaching keep that might as well be a city in its own right. Buildings painted vibrant colors like purple and even pink circled the main keep all the way to the coastline and even beyond... a boardwalk supported by poles that plunged into the shallow waters also held houses and shops above the waters.

The tower of Tortuga itself was an elaborate sight that commanded attention, even from a distance. Unlike the castle at Navarre, Tortuga had the look of an exquisite palace, constructed from what looked to be white stone almost as vibrant as the snow that painted the landscape, gradually narrowing from the base to the top with a pointed purple roof adorned by a silver disc.

"An astrolabe, if you are wondering," Ahmin said

conversationally, no doubt following the angle of Sunay's head. "It was supposedly a gift from one of Domina Morgana's peers upon founding of her tower, but I suspect she commissioned it herself. The Domina *is* quite vain."

Sunay forced herself not to look back and make eye contact with the admiral, which Ahmin noticed. "Why are acting like I'm about to gut you and throw you overboard?

The foxgirl admitted, "Uhh... I dunno? Just a bit unnerved that it's jus' the two of us."

The admiral made a throaty chuckle. "Sunay, if you ever disappoint me, let me assure you that there will be no doubt that you have done so. I am not a subtle man, either in stature or manner."

Sunay finally had the courage to turn around to face him. "Then... can I ask what we're doin' here?"

"We have business with Domina Morgana, though she requested to see you specifically."

"Me? How would she even know about me? And what could she want me for?"

Ahmin shook his head. "The Domina has a way of knowing things she shouldn't know, which concerns me to some small degree. As for what she wants you for, I suspect she could explain her motives far better than I could guess. Don't worry, I won't be leaving you alone with her."

"Would that be a problem?" Sunay asked.

"One never knows with that woman."

The shallows became *very* shallow, to the point where Sunay could clearly see the bottom despite the clay tainting the water. While Tortuga didn't rest on some high cliff or bluff, this was no sandy coastline either. It was a dirty muck, just like everything else in northern Avalon.

It felt colder on the rowboat than it did on the deck of the *Goldbeard*, and Sunay became acutely aware of her own icy breath as it escaped her lips. Ahmin didn't seem bothered by the cold... but then again, Ahmin never seemed bothered by anything. But at least he looked appropriately dressed for once.

Ice was the bane of ships, but at the speed they were going, the danger wasn't nearly as significant, even as the chunks grew thicker the closer they got to the ice shelf. The common knowledge was that no snowflake was the same, but Sunay found the same could be true for any given piece of ice. Some were a murky white, or streaked with red, brown, and even green. Some were round and some were jagged.

Some floated harmlessly on top of the water, others only showed a finger above the surface and hid a ship destroying monster beneath.

But ice around Tortuga was different still... the pieces she saw were clear as crystal, and some smaller pieces actually had sharp edges and facets like a jewel, and refracted the sunlight above into rainbows that splayed out on the side of the boat. Even if Sunay hadn't known one of the world's most powerful mages held court in this very keep, she would have guessed the area was magical.

The sight was so breathtaking that she didn't even realize the boat had reached the "dock" until it bumped against the boards and jerked to a stop. A heavily bundled soldier, with furs dyed blue draped over silvery chain mail came to assist, tossing a thick mooring rope to Ahmin that they used to secure the boat to the dock.

The soldier assisted Sunay onto the boardwalk, even though she didn't particularly need it, and offered a similar hand to Ahmin that was refused. "You got here in just in time," the soldier said. "Too much longer and you'd probably have needed to walk across the ice."

Ahmin noted, "The ocean doesn't normally freeze this far, as I recall."

"We've had some cold winters the last two years. It concerns all of us."

"Surely Tortuga prepares for harsh winter."

"*We* do, yes. We can also get supplies from the south if we're willing to pay the tax. But our 'friends' up north don't have that luxury. Too many rough winters in a row means they get more and more willing to come south and take what they need. If we don't get milder and shorter winters soon, we could see another Daynish Campaign."

Ahmin scoffed. "Not even the most desperate Dayne would think Tortuga a viable target. I can assure you they haven't stopped singing tales of the night the sky cried fire and ice. "

Sunay's ears twitched at the idea of a tale she hadn't heard yet. She had grown keen on such stories since leaving Miriam's orphanage.

Ahmin also knew what that reaction meant, and he laughed before saying, "In the best of times, Tortuga sits well within the borders of Avalon. But the northern border of the kingdom and now republic is an oft changing thing. The last time the line shifted was nearly seventeen years ago, at the height of the last Daynish Campaigns. The money and manpower Avalon spent to fight off the invaders drove most of the population into poverty and prompted the revolution shortly after. That part you should know."

He motioned for her to follow as he moved down the

boardwalk, continuing the story as they began their trek to the keep. "It was during that period, at the deepest thrust of the invasion, that the Daynes made their first, and only, attempt on Tortuga. The Chieftain Hrothkin roused ten thousand of his people to lay siege on the somewhat fledgling keep founded by the Domina. She was not pleased.

"She went out alone to hear the chief's demands for tribute, then offered but one of her own. 'I will spare one man to tell the rest of your kind what happened to you pathetic lot.' As Hrothkin laughed, the Domina raised her arms to the heavens... and sent the sky crashing down.

"To the east of here, in the stretch of plain that is now called Morgana's Wrath, balls of flaming rock and spears of icy slate decimated the land and all that stood upon it. At the end of the cataclysm, only two remained standing: the Domina and an unnamed Dayne that she spared to tell the tale to his people. Since that time, even when the Daynes have pushed the border south, they have given Tortuga a wide berth."

"And now I see why you wouldn't want me alone wit' her," Sunay said with a shiver. "Sounds like she's the sorta girl that could even hurt *you*."

Ahmin laughed. It was hard to tell just how much the tales from the *Goldbeard's* crew of the Admiral's invulnerability were true and how much of it was stretched. Ahmin himself never confirmed or denied them, but Sunay had already seen him survive enough things that should have rightfully killed him to never doubt such stories. "Let's say that I have no desire whatsoever to test that theory. Morgana is arguably the most powerful mortal being on this continent, even among her peers. Not even I would try her willingly."

At the end of the boardwalk they entered the city proper, and Sunay imagined that she had stepped twenty years back in time. Until the Revolution inspired a more low-key, functional, and practical appearance, all the major cities in Northern Avalon looked like this, colorful and even garish with colors that should never have been next to each other like purple and orange for the three story house they just passed with a bright pink roof.

Sunay also became keenly aware that she was drawing attention from passers-by, older men and women specifically stopping to give her a double take. As a member of the Gold Pirates, and specifically under Admiral Ahmin's command, she had no fear of displaying her chimera traits even in public, and had gotten used to the stares she got from doing so. But this was different, she was getting pointed to and quiet mumbling amongst themselves.

As much as she wanted to demand to know just what they thought they were looking at, Sunay stilled her tongue. Even if she had the protection of her crew, it was a tenuous allowance where her presence was more tolerated than accepted. Picking fights wouldn't be prudent. Instead, she stewed over the quiet gossiping and tried to keep her head forward as much as possible.

They stopped at the inner wall of Tortuga, which formed a perfect circle and separated the central tower from the rest of the city, and the soldiers there were less welcoming than the one at the dock. They were two large men with full helmets that obscured their facial features, even their eyes barely visible through the small slit afforded.

"State your business," the one on the left said. If he was trying to be intimidating, it wouldn't be easy to do so considering he was still dwarfed by the towering pirate admiral.

"We were summoned by the Domina," Ahmin retorted. "You should ask her."

"Names?"

"Ahmin and Sunay. We are expected."

The soldier to the right of the gate turned the corner, and examined a white slab hanging from a hook. He then nodded to his companion, and motioned to someone through the gate, causing the steel grate to slowly raise. "Mind your manners, buccaneer. The Domina might be in a mood," he warned courteously.

"Isn't she always?" Ahmin scoffed, then motioned for Sunay to fall in step as the gate gave enough clearance for them to enter.

The inner courtyard was covered in a blanket of snow, with only the skeletons of trees serving as a reminder that anything grew there. From this closer vantage point, Sunay could now see that the blocks that made the tower was actually white marble. "Whelp, that couldn't have been cheap," she remarked, pointing at the stones.

Ahmin agreed. "No, I doubt it was, especially since those sorts of quarries are only found in the Free Provinces to the east. And that marble needs to be carved in a specific way in order for mortar to take hold, which would be an added expense. As I mentioned, the Domina is quite vain."

There weren't any soldiers at the tower doors, which Sunay found peculiar, as everywhere else seemed to be teeming with uniformed men. *All* of them men, now that she thought about it. Even the Republican Army realized they needed women to fill their ranks nowadays.

The front door opened seemingly on its own, as there wasn't a soul anywhere inside that could have done it as far as Sunay could see. The two pirates stepped onto a circular landing with a mosaic pattern of an astrolabe on the floor. It appeared that the landing was the entire floor, in fact, as she could see windows with sunlight pouring in all around the circumference.

The foxgirl's head jerked upwards when she heard a grinding and clicking sound from the ceiling, heralding a golden circular staircase spinning down until it touched the landing floor at the center of the astrolabe with a click. It was followed by a light, melodic voice saying, "If only my traders and diplomats were as punctual as a buccaneer."

The clack of high heeled shoes rang down from above, belonging to the dainty violet shoes that appeared on the golden steps. It was followed by a woman in a dark purple dress trimmed with silver and adorned with sapphires cut low in the chest to accentuate an impressive line of cleavage. A silver tiara adorned her forehead, encrusted with sapphires, aquamarines, and diamonds. Alabaster skin and long, waist length hair as black as coal completed the picture of the traditional image of Avalonian beauty, if not for the fact that she was close to six feet tall even *without* the heels.

"Being on time is essential for a proper society. I am sorry your associates do not share that sentiment."

The woman offered her hand palm down, and Ahmin took it with a respectful bow. "Domina Morgana, this is Sunay, the member of my crew you asked about."

Everything about the Domina's manner was polite and respectful, but there was something about the mage that made Sunay's skin crawl. Perhaps it was that Morgana could not be as young as she looked, and was using *some* manner of magic to appear so radiant.

Or perhaps it was because the Domina sounded so nice while her eyes sized up the foxgirl like she was a thick slab of steak. "A pleasure to meet you, my dear," Morgana said with a knowing smile. "I must say, the fox is my favorite animal. The red fox, specifically, not those dreadfully bland gray ones down south. I can now see why Cavalier Norman took interest in you."

Sunay asked, "You knew 'bout that?"

"After the fact, but yes. Do understand, I was the one who applied the chimeric curse upon the king, on behest of the queen after they were married. She didn't wish any challenges to the throne, and I did not much like the king. I chose the red fox for that curse. That was no doubt why you were his target, though how he learned about you, I do not know."

Sunay's eyes flared. "Are you tellin' me that I'm some bastard daughter of the king?"

Morgana shrugged. "That is impossible to say. I was hardly the only mage who cast a chimeric curse for some coin, and I doubt I was the only one who used the red fox as inspiration. But sadly Norman, by my experience, does not think of such details, and seeks only to please the zealous Coders of his imagination and the Parliament that didn't string him up with the nobility that did not escape its ire."

Sunay sensed there was a lie somewhere tucked into that entire exchange, but couldn't put a finger on where.

The Domina turned about on the ball of her right foot, and said, "But that is not why I summoned you, my dear. And fear not, my fine Admiral, I have something for you as well in exchange."

Morgana returned to the stairwell, and glanced back with a sweet, apologetic smile, "I do apologize for not inviting you up. There was a bit of an incident recently, and I'm afraid to say that the rest of the tower is still not suitable for hosting guests."

She twiddled her fingers as she climbed the steps, and furnishings appeared from the thin air around the two pirates, a pair of large red velvet and mahogany chairs behind them, and a long luxurious couch of the same materials in front of them. "Do sit down, darlings," she said, disappearing into the higher floor. "I shall be back shortly."

Sunay shuddered as she sat. Everything about that woman gave her chills. This entire damn place gave her chills. A cold, clammy feeling that spread down her spine to her toes.

"I can promise you that she is watching us," Ahmin warned. "And probably listening too."

With that in mind, Sunay straightened as stiff as a board, and determined to not move unless asked, and not speak unless spoken to.

The Domina returned ten minutes later, a tan book under her arm and that same pleasant and unnerving smile upon her face. "I apologize for the delay. I must admit to being dreadfully unprepared with all the goings-on."

Ahmin queried, "You mentioned there was an incident. Is there some way we could help?"

Sunay knew that the admiral wasn't offering any assistance for the sake of good relations. Something had happened, and he wanted to know more.

Morgana also seemed to know that. "Nothing that has not already been handled. A troublesome apprentice that I had to deal with. He merely caused an unholy mess of things in the process."

"That would explain the lack of any other living things in the tower," Ahmin noted.

The veil fell for just a moment from the Domina's face, and the anger behind it was evident. "I only allow those I trust in my tower. If I cannot trust anyone, no one enters."

Ahmin smiled visibly through his mask. "And yet here we are."

That gave Morgana the opportunity to reconstruct the pleasant mask. "Yes, that you are. I do not believe that trust is misplaced, no?"

"I would hope not. We've always had an amiable working relationship."

Morgana grinned almost predatorily, and lay down in a blatantly suggestive manner across the couch, setting her book down on the floor, with her right hand lying across the curve on her thigh, and her left propping up her chin so as to allow a good line of sight down the low neckline of her dress. "The extent of which is *always* up for negotiation."

Sunay cringed, despite her efforts not to. Those were mental images she didn't need. The foxgirl wondered how many men would have fallen to the Domina's charms and never been seen again.

"As many women who befell the same fate, my dear," Morgana replied with a playful wink, startling Sunay into worrying she had expressed her thoughts unwittingly out loud.

Could the Domina read minds?

Admiral Ahmin and Domina Morgana both said at the same time, "No" and "Yes" respectively, which offered no help at all for the foxgirl's nerves.

The large pirate leaned forward, his voice dropping out of pleasantness and into stern. "Domina, my time is valuable, as is yours. May I ask what business you have with us today?"

Morgana moved the fingers of her right hand, and the book in front of her flapped open, several pages flying out onto a breeze no one could feel towards the large pirate admiral, who plucked them out of the air. She locked eyes with Sunay. "Daynish movements over the last month, and I know you've had trouble keeping agents alive that far north. There's also some information from my continuing Void research that might have some value to you. Hasn't amounted to much for me."

"Not as keen on the 'grand mission' as your peers?"

Morgana huffed. "We have differences in opinion. But *that* is little of your concern. My 'peers' do not particularly like you or your organization, and I should maintain that confidence. Besides, I am more interested in the young lady here."

Sunay gulped as the Domina's eyes bore holes into hers.

"I have been interested in 'chosen' people for some time, but I rarely get the opportunity to talk to one."

"You... you've 'eard about my being chosen?" Sunay asked nervously.

Morgana nodded slowly. "Oh yes, my dear. And not all who are 'chosen' go into the Admiral's care here. They are all taken by... something... that guides them in whatever direction it wishes, an inner voice that sounds like them, feels like them, yet *isn't* them. Would you say you had a similar experience?"

Sunay looked towards Ahmin for guidance, and the pirate admiral said, "Answer. It's okay."

The foxgirl nodded. "Yes. When I was... runnin' from Cavalier Norman and 'is mob, there was somethin' that... pulled me towards Admiral Ahmin. When I resisted, I lost control of my body until I complied."

"Normally, the calling from that inner voice is so subtle that those who have been chosen never realize their actions aren't their own,; but sometimes, like in your case, the pull is more extreme. I must know, can you think of any other time where your actions have been inconsistent with what you would have done?"

Sunay shook her head. "I really couldn't say. I... always kinda been a random sort."

The answer appeared more helpful than Sunay figured it would be. "Interesting," Morgana almost purred. "Where are you from initially?"

"I had lived in the orphanage outside of Navarre for as long as I can remember."

Morgana pushed herself up to a sitting position, then stood. "That's all the questions I had. As sudden as it may seem, I do have so very much to do, and I'm sure you'd rather get your crew as south as possible before the worst of winter hits."

Ahmin followed, accepting Morgana's hand for another bow. "I do, actually. Thank you for this information, Domina. I hope your coming days have fewer... incidents."

"As do I.  Farewell, Admiral.  Sunay.  May the Coders bless your steps."

Morgana retreated back to the higher floors, the stairwell rising behind her, as the pirates retreated from the keep and back towards their ship.

Sunay cast wary glances back towards the keep before asking, "And what was *that* little interrogation about?  Do ya know?"

Ahmin was dividing his attention between the papers in front of him and making sure he didn't run over anyone as he walked. Nonetheless, he answered. "Domina Morgana has a bit of a theory that I think might have some merit.  She thinks that the number of 'chosen' people has been diminishing over the years, and thinks that it is somehow correlated to the advance of the Void as it has devoured the rest of the world."

Sunay cocked her head.  "And 'ow does *that* figure?"

"Unlike Morgana, I actually *know* just how many chosen there are, and she's right; there *are* fewer than there were fifty years ago, or even ten years ago.  I don't know if it's coincidence, or even *how* it would correlate, but there may be unexpected fruit to find there.  I'm inclined to let the Domina pursue it."

"And that's why you brought me here then?"

Ahmin tossed aside the papers he had been holding with a shrug. "It's not like I didn't know the stuff she gave me already.  The Daynes aren't all that hard to figure out, and I have been given no reason to interfere in those affairs."

"So we came all this way for no reason but to have that... witch... make me feel like worms were eatin' my bones?"

"No.  I rather like this part of the world.  I have no problems taking excuses to come up this way, especially in winter.  I spent most of my life in tropical climates.  The cold and the snow are a welcome change of pace.  And if I'm being rather honest, I rather *like* Domina Morgana, as self-absorbed and insufferable as she can be."

"You just like her chest," Sunay snorted.

"It *is* impressive, but I've seen better."

It was unusual to see the pirate admiral so lighthearted, choosing a very no nonsense demeanor whenever he addressed his crew or other public scenarios.  It made her smile that he let his guard down around her.

"*What?*  I have," he insisted, mistaking Sunay's appraisal for disbelief.

Sunay shook her head, and said, "No, that's not... oh never

mind. Let's git back to the ship."

~ ~ ~ ~ ~

"Nice work, Sunay! You're already gettin' the hang of the sails!"

Sunay looked down at Juno. Not even two months ago, seeing all six of those red eyes gleaming at her would have caused her to shiver. But meeting Domina Morgana in her self-imposed isolation had given the foxgirl a new definition of "creepy." After that, Juno's beady stare was nothing.

"Thanks! I had a good teacher!" she called down, checking to make sure she had tied the knot as well as Juno claimed. "But I don't think I'm ever gonna be able to do all this without a 'arness like ya can!"

She had only started learning the role of rigger last week, though she would have liked warmer waters to try it in. The frigid climate of the Western Forever Sea off of the Daynelands was *not* what Sunay considered ideal conditions, especially since working with rope meant she couldn't even wear gloves. Her fingers were already blue long before she dropped back down to the deck.

She blew air into her hands, even though she knew that wouldn't help in the long run. Moist air from her lungs would make her hands feel warmer for a little bit, then the moisture would dry and her hands would feel *colder.*

"Ya shouldn't do that," Juno warned.

Sunay snapped back, "I think yer teachin' me the rigging 'cause you don't wanna do it in this cold."

The spidergirl smiled and tilted her head playfully. "Ya got it in one!"

"Gloves... need gloves..." Sunay grumbled, and turned about to find Jacques holding two black woolen mittens in front of her face. With a gleeful expression, the foxgirl grabbed them and thrust both hands into blissful insulation.

"Admiral on the deck!" Bolin declared in full yell, stirring the rest of the crew to turn as Ahmin emerged from below.

"I have received orders from the Administrators. We are shipping off to warmer waters."

That got a hearty cheer, even from Sunay, though she still didn't know exactly what to think about these unseen "Administrators" that supposedly governed an entire shadow network both on land and by sea, or how Admiral Ahmin got those orders.

"Where we goin', Admiral?" Bolin asked.

Ahmin frowned. He either didn't like where they were going, didn't want to leave here, or both. "We're going to the South Forever Sea, monitoring The Imperial Aramathea, the eastern portion of the empire specifically. There's apparently some trouble brewing there, and reports that the Void might be shifting."

The cheers turned to concern. The Void hadn't shown any signs of movement in about three decades, since it consumed the continent of Xanadu and half of the Eastern Forever Sea. There was only one way it could move at this point, and that caused dread to sink upon the crew. Sunay knew these things from the various tales of her crewmates, but didn't *know* it, she hadn't *seen* the Void first hand like many of her comrades had.

And Admiral Ahmin guessed as much. He approached Sunay, and looked down at her, his eyes narrowing to slits. "Sunay hasn't had the pleasure of seeing dire water yet, has she?" he said.

"No, sir," Jacques replied. "We've not had that duty since she came aboard."

The Admiral ordered to the helm, "I think we have time for one slight detour, then. Bolin! 270 degrees, full sail. Juno! I'll need your eyes on the crow's nest! Send Balco down to manage the sails!"

"Aye aye, Admiral!" the spidergirl answered, shimmying up the main mast.

Sunay was puzzled by the change in duties, and Ahmin explained. "Balco has the keenest sight I have ever seen, but in this case Juno's eyes allow her to catch the subtle differences in the water that can mean living to see tomorrow and sailing into oblivion. It *should* be at least a full day's sail to reach the end of the living world, but *if* the rumors are true, I don't want to take any chances that it hasn't advanced from the west as well."

The mercy was that the line *hadn't* moved by the time that they heard Juno's cry of, "Dire water! Dead ahead, half mile out!"

But that really didn't help Sunay any, because she felt a cold chill shoot down her back, and the fur on her tail sticking straight on end. Her ears flattened and she began to cower. This was *not* a pleasant feeling at all, like invisible hands were grabbing her by the spine and twisting.

Balco noticed that, and laughed. "Admiral! Lookit the greenhorn!"

Ahmin did, and his reaction was not humor. "Sunay... you can *feel* the dire water nearby, can't you?"

"Is *that* what this feelin' is?" she said with a shiver, one that she wished she could blame on the chilly air and waters of the Western Forever Sea.

Ahmin put his hands on her shoulders, and said reassuringly, "To have this sense is rare, Sunay. It's always hardest the first time you experience it. As you get used to the presence of dire water, it doesn't affect you as badly."

The towering pirate gently pushed Sunay to the port side and ordered out to the helm, "Bring us alongside the water line, Bolin. Balco, keep the sails full. Jacques, ready the oarsmen to help push us off when I give the word."

Sunay figured out why the oarsmen would be needed as the *Goldbeard* turned. There were normally very strong winds in the open sea, but here the air movement died to a breeze and went stagnant. The smell changed to something that Sunay wouldn't describe as death, but more lacking life... a sterile and empty scent that gave her shivers all over again.

Ahmin had to effectively *carry* Sunay to the railing because her legs began to refuse going any closer, every muscle stiffening in reluctance and fear. Once there he pointed out to the west, and asked, "Can you see the difference? It's near impossible unless you're up close or can see heat like Juno. But once you see it, there's no mistake."

The foxgirl couldn't initially, until Ahmin instructed her towards the proper location. To someone who didn't know any better, the transition would be similar to how shallow waters broke into deep waters from the shoreline. It was not a phenomenon one expected to see while out in the open seas. The already deep blue turned to something darker, something not blue nor black, an impossible color that Sunay couldn't quite wrap her mind around.

But once she could see the difference, she found herself horrified that she didn't see it sooner. The dire water didn't move. There were no waves on the surface, and an ominous purple mist hovered over it. It was like Ahmin had pulled away an invisible curtain, and what lurked behind was a featureless horror.

Ahmin turned his head towards the aft side. "Joffe, you have one of your candles on the deck somewhere?"

The scholar sighed in resignation, but retrieved the five inch rocket he had been toying with on the starboard side, attached it to a leader, and handed it over to the admiral. "Even if they are one use only, seems like a waste to use it here," he said forlornly.

Normally, rockets like those were pointed upwards, and were used for nearby Gold Pirate ships to relay positions or distress among themselves quickly. Ahmin pointed this one almost parallel to the water, aiming towards the dire water ahead, then lit the wick.

At the end of the wick, the rocket zipped off the leader with a crackling hiss, then took off at unnatural speed and with uncanny accuracy towards the water boundary... then disintegrated. Not with the telltale pop and colorful burst that she had come to expect, but with nothing. No flourish, no sound... merely fell apart and vaporized, even the white smoke trail vanishing like an invisible hand had chopped it clean, swallowed by the purple mist of the Void.

"That is what the Void does, it consumes and leaves nothing but dire water behind. Nothing that crosses that line is ever seen again," Ahmin said softly into Sunay's ear. "And that is also one of our primary duties out on the water... to monitor the dire water, and to manage evacuations of areas that are in the way of its advance."

The pirate admiral turned about, and barked with such volume that it could be heard on the lower decks, "Get those oars moving!"

The volume of the order rang in Sunay's ears, and the steady movement away from dire water shook her mind out of its frozen state, as if her thoughts and her muscles were slowly defrosting and starting to work properly again, helped as the invisible curtain of sanity was pulled back over the sea, and the Void was again invisible to her gaze. She shuddered once more to work out all the kinks, and absentmindedly started smoothing out her tail.

That wasn't the first time she had felt that icy clench in her bones. She had felt something very similar in Tortuga, specifically in Domina Morgana's tower, but even she didn't think that made much sense. It certainly wasn't something she wanted to air openly with the crew present. Even with their experience with the Void, she could see the tension when the admiral ordered them to sail this way. They didn't like being here either, they were just better at not letting it bother them.

The admiral *did* say that she was welcome to approach him with *any* concerns she had... but would he willing be receptive to an accusation about something that he had declared a certain degree of respect for?

"What's on your mind, Sunay?"

The foxgirl jerked in fright, spinning about to see Ahmin looking straight at her. She wasn't exactly sure how to answer because she wasn't even sure what questions she wanted to ask. Apparently, she hadn't been masking her uncertainty very well.

Ahmin turned his head towards the aft side below the helm, where the stairwell to the lower decks was located behind a door. After reluctant silent deliberation, he ordered, "Follow me. We'll talk in my quarters."

Sunay followed the admiral as he pulled open the door and ducked down into the lower decks. Even on a ship as large as the *Goldbeard*, there wasn't much head room for people of average stature. Ahmin had to traverse the halls nearly doubled over and with his shoulders drawn in. If someone was trying to go the opposite way, Admiral Ahmin wasn't going to be the one to back up.

Fortunately for the massive pirate, his cabin was much more accommodating due to the fact that he had knocked out the entire floor above. It was good to be the man in charge, as his personal space was at three times that of anyone else's... although having *any* room to herself would be better that the cot and footlocker she had now.

Although she'd hardly call Ahmin's cabin palatial either... his bed, while large, was of exceptionally plain oak, as were the table, chairs, and standing closet. The only thing that really stuck out as unusual was a small black iron cabinet with an open padlock and chain on the aft wall sitting on a shelf.

He straightened to his full height with a sigh of relief, then hastily rushed to the oak table in the center, covering up something with his body that Sunay didn't get a chance to see. He then took whatever it was, and put it in the iron cabinet before pulling the chain tight and locking it closed.

Ahmin offered the most unbelieving of explanations. "Apologies, I hadn't bothered to tidy up because I wasn't expecting to host anyone."

Sunay closed her eyes. "I didn't see anythin'. Honest. One of those things I'm not supposed to know about, eh?"

"Not yet," he answered cryptically, "but that is a discussion for a later time. Seeing the dire water really shook you, didn't it? I am sorry... but it is one of our primary purposes out on the seas. You were going to have to face it at some point."

Sunay shook her head. "It's not that. I... I've felt that way before."

*That* got Ahmin's attention, as Sunay should not have had any prior experience with the Void. "Where?"

"When we were in Domina Morgana's tower. Not nearly as strong, but the same sort of clammy feelin'. At the time, I thought she just creeped me out. But..."

Ahmin cursed under his breath and mumbled, “Had I known sooner...” then he quickly added when Sunay cringed in guilt, “It's *not* your fault. You couldn't have known. Domina Morgana no doubt has been playing with the Void, and had I suspected so at the time, I could have applied some pressure and found out exactly *what* that 'incident' she spoke of entailed. I'm going to have to pass this on... our orders are clear.”

Sunay could sense his displeasure. “You don't like that.”

“I... do not have a particularly high opinion of the Administrator that has been tasked to watch this region, no. But he is an established member with holdings in the area, and I am mobile by nature. So I go, and he stays.”

The admiral sighed, then admitted, “I don't disagree with the orders, though. Domina Morgana *might* be playing around with powers she can't control. But we *know* that things are going to get hot in the south for the next few years. The Gold Pirates need to be there in force to make sure events flow smoothly.”

“Anything specific you can tell me yet?”

Ahmin shook his head. “You will know shortly after I do.”

“If that was meant to be reassurin', it didn't work,” Sunay said flatly.

“It wasn't meant to be.”

“Wonderful...”

# Chapter Seven: Good News First

Warmer weather was always welcome, no matter how much Sunay's red fox heritage would suggest she should be comfortable in the cold of Northern Avalon. So, the foxgirl certainly didn't have any problems whatsoever once her homeland was in the aft, and a rest of the continent was in the fore.

Admiral Ahmin had ordered her to become more familiar with all of the crew and their responsibilities, even though Sunay couldn't understand why. She was hardly a weakling, but there was no way she'd be able to pull her weight on the oars, and everyone down on that deck knew it.

"We're in free waters now, lassie," Gurgn said after telling the rowing team to withdraw their oars. They had hit the ocean currents that would take them to the southern empire of The Imperial Aramathea far faster than they could row, even with southern winds heralding the coming spring.

Gurgn was a thick heavy-set man with arms like legs and legs like tree trunks, and even he considered himself too old to be able to handle the duties, hence his position at the head of the procession calling out the cadence of the team's strokes. But it was the admiral's orders to get to know them and what they did, so she was there watching.

"And yer point?" the foxgirl said tiredly, with her chin in her hands.

"You've never been outside of Avalon, until now."

"Yer point?"

Gurgn exhaled sharply. "Why don't you go topside and see this brand new world around you?"

Sunay merely turned her eyes in the rowmaster's direction. "Ya sure?"

"We're not complex folk to figure out. If ya wanna visit, we won't stop ya, but for today, get up there."

Sunay smiled slightly, and nearly skipped to the stairwell. She knew that the sea off of the Free Provinces wouldn't be any different than the waters of Southern Avalon, but it certainly *felt* fresher and the sky a little brighter once she stepped out onto the deck, and took a deep breath.

The day was in truth partly cloudy, which wasn't terribly

surprising, those clouds being the harbinger of the spring storms that would soon sweep over this part of the continent. Memories of those storms actually got her worried. "Hey! What're we gonna do if a cyclone hits on the water?"

Admiral Ahmin spun about, looking up from the map he was holding. "Sunay! How very fortuitous. I was about to call for you. As for the weather, cyclones aren't much of a worry the further south we go. By the time the really big storm fronts hit this area, we'll be in Aramathea."

Jacques snorted, and added, "We'll only have to worry about typhoons down there."

That didn't sound any better at all to Sunay's ears.

Ahmin playfully pushed his first mate away, which had the effect of knocking Jacques off his feet and face-planting him on the deck. "Anyway, I was going to call for you because we're making one quick stop in the coast city of Beredon, and I'd like for you to attend me."

"Arr?" Sunay growled, tilting her head with curiosity.

"We're getting a little bit of shore leave, but there's somewhere I want to show you," he said unhelpfully.

The foxgirl was understandably skeptical. "The last time ya wanted to show me somethin' I found myself starin' at the Void."

The large pirate's mask shifted as his lips turned upward, and he closed his eyes playfully. "I think you'll find this surprise much less harrowing."

She had no reason not to believe him. Ahmin hadn't ever lied to her before, after all. But that didn't mean she was entirely buying whatever he was selling. "Uh huh."

"Beredon docks, two miles!" Balco shouted.

Juno added in, "Two hundred feet. We should be good and clear to the docks!"

"Then bring us in, Bolin," Ahmin said. "Jacques, make sure the rowers are ready to help slow us down, then have Gurgn drop anchor."

Beredon was the primary port for the entire free province of Catalan, which like most Free Provinces was more of a loose association of independent city-states than an organized body. Due to this unique status, the city had a dockside roughly three times larger than the city itself, and large enough for the *Goldbeard* itself to moor to.

"Alright, ladies and gentlemen, as you well know, there are

less savory pirates that use this port as well," Ahmin declared as the crew assembled on the deck to be dismissed. "Some of you may even meet old friends here. Regardless, I must insist that you behave professionally. If you get drunk, you're in the brig for a week. If you start a fight, you're in the brig for two. And if you so much as think of participating in any despicable behavior like your ragamuffin kin, consider yourself lucky if I merely decide to *leave* you here. We are Gold Pirates, and we are *above* such base behavior. Am I understood?"

The crew called out their agreement in near unison.

"As always, First Mate Jacques has a duty roster for watching the ship while we are in port. You *will* follow it. I will *know* if you don't. I and Crewman Sunay will return in three days, and we will cast off at high sun." The Admiral then smiled, and said, "And with all those unpleasant restrictions out of the way, go have fun, my friends. You've earned it. *Dismissed!*"

With a loud cheer, the crew initially tried to rush forward before the first mate quickly restored order and imposed a line for the crew to disembark. Ahmin's grin cracked even further, to the point that Sunay could almost see his cheekbones rise over the fold of his mask.

"I have a good crew," he explained upon seeing Sunay's quizzical expression. "Not everyone can say that, even among my peers in the Gold Pirates. It does me joy to see them so happy."

"We're all clear, Admiral," Jacques said, approaching the pair. "Bolin and I will head the first watch, and you are free to depart. We'll see ya in three days."

Ahmin offered his hand, and the pair shook on it. "Yes, you will. Don't forget to have a little bit of fun yourself."

"I will, in the wee hours of the morning after all my old friends are long since passed out in their rum glasses."

The admiral and first mate laughed, and Ahmin used that as parting to head down the gangplank to the dockside, Sunay falling in step behind him. Ahmin glanced over his shoulder, and said, "We won't linger here... because I think you're going to want to spend some considerable time at our destination, and if we leave now we should get there come late evening."

"That long of a walk?" Sunay asked.

"Walk? If we were to walk, it'd take the whole three days one way. We're going to get some assistance to get where we're going."

The assistance in this case turned out to be the back of a partially loaded merchant's cart headed towards Terrasa, a nearby city-state to the north. Ahmin offered the husband and wife couple a substantial sum to ride in the back, which the husband was reluctant to take until his wife arrived carrying a bushel of apples from the market.

The merchant's wife was a chimera, with a beautiful gray wolf tail and pointed ears that instantly turned in Sunay's direction. "Oh, Law, do stop being such a louse and let these people ride with us. It's not like we don't have the space and we can always use the extra coin."

"They have the look of pirates," Law countered suspiciously.

"Good, then they'll ward off any bandits that think us an easy mark."

The woman stopped in front of Sunay, and the foxgirl immediately sensed something different about the wolfgirl. She smelled too much like a wolf and not nearly enough like a human. It was entirely odd. "I'm Rola, and you are?"

"Sunay..."

"Charmed," Rola replied, then looked down at the basket in her arms and squeaked in surprise. "I do apologize! I'd offer you more suitable greetings, but I forgot I picked these up for the trip. I do *so* love apples. Do be quick and get on board, we'd like to make Terrasa by evening."

Ahmin climbed into the back, and was about to offer Sunay a hand when Rola interrupted. "Oh goodness, no! It will not do to have such a sweet girl getting jostled and bumped around. Come up front with Law and me. I promise we don't bite."

Law scoffed. "*I* don't, at the very least."

Rola glared, and replied, "Only when you *ask* for it, love."

Rola slid all the way to Law's side as he took the reins of their single horse cart, and motioned for Sunay to take the seat next to her. "You're going to have me holding the reins from the end of..." Law began to protest, then sighed before his wife could even respond. "Yes. Of course you are."

With the riders situated, the cart began its trip down the tributary road off the Great Trade Line that led towards Terrasa. "You have the smell of Avalon on you," Rola said knowingly. "Born there, I assume?"

Sunay nodded, on guard with the attentions of this woman. The foxgirl just couldn't figure out the conflicting messages her senses were getting. "Yeah."

"I spent a lot of time there. Had to wear silly hats and long skirts *all the time*. Make no mistake, I *love* silly hats and long skirts, but when that's *all* you can wear because people would lose their minds if they saw you... ugh. And of course, they're the country who *created* most of them with their dreadful curses... ugh! Create 'em and hate 'em, makes *no* sense, don't you think?"

At least Sunay could agree with that. "No, it doesn't. I take it you're *not* from Avalon, then?"

Rola shook her head animatedly, her long coppery hair causing Law to wince as it slapped him in the face. "Nope. I was born far to the north, in the Daynelands, actually. Not that they liked me all that much up *there* by the time I came home, either."

Sunay had a hard time taking that at face value. "You don't look much like a Dayne."

"No, I really don't, do I?" Rola replied with the sort of grin that made Sunay want to jump right off the cart and scramble high up the nearest tree. "Spent five years trying to find my way back home to discover my home wanted to sacrifice me to the Winter Walkers beyond the Icy Wastes. Coders, what a mess *that* was. Winter Walkers. Pfeh! Absurd!"

Ahmin started laughing, though Sunay really couldn't think of what was all that funny. When the foxgirl leaned around to give him a good solid silent angry stare, he said, "Daynish behavior has always amused me. It'd be *really* funny if it didn't sometimes lead to massive amounts of bloodshed."

Meanwhile, Rola quickly concluded her tale. "But fortunately, I had Law with me, and despite his frail looks and meager strength..."

"Hey..." her husband protested meekly.

"He is also remarkably cunning, and shuffled me away from that terrible place and terrible people. Now, we travel back and forth on these small roads with mostly peaceful people, where I can display my traits without fear. I like it. It helps that I'm hardly the only one like me. A lot of chimeras have settled in this area, especially around Terrasa. I almost feel like a *majority* in that town."

A city of chimeras? Sunay had to admit that *did* sound appealing.

"We simply *must* have drinks in Terrasa!" Rola exclaimed happily, taking Sunay's hands in hers.

Ahmin laughed again, and said, "I suspect we won't have time for that... we both have somewhere to be, and don't have too much time to spare if we want to return promptly."

"Oh," Rola said, not hiding her disappointment. "Well, if we are heading your way, you are always welcome to hop in the back to get there."

Sunay sincerely hoped that didn't happen, at least not until she figured out just what felt so off about this woman. The foxgirl still couldn't figure out if Rola wanted to hug her, eat her, or both.

Ahmin finally let her in on the mystery when they finally parted ways with the two merchants at the town square of Terrasa, Ahmin leading Sunay north while Law and Rola went east. "I wonder if that man Law knows why he's going to have a lot of little wolf chimeras running around in the near future."

"I can't imagine why he wouldn't," Sunay replied. "Chimeric curses can linger for generations. Ol' Kaeli back at my orphanage was the result of her great-grandpa fooling around with one his wife's handmaidens."

"True, but that's not what I meant. The Daynes used to pay homage to the animal spirits of the north, like the spirit wolves. It was only recently, after the last Daynish Campaigns twenty some odd years ago, that they started worshiping the Winter Walkers, which are believed to be the ghosts of famed Daynish Kings of the past. Just recently, the story started spreading that if spirits of the land were sacrificed to the Winter Walkers, that they wouldn't freeze the north in harsh winter."

"Oh," Sunay said, then it clicked. "Ohhhhhhh... *that's* why she smelled odd to me. She wasn't a chimera at all."

"Indeed. And I wonder if Law *truly* understands that."

"Why?"

The pirate admiral chuckled. "Because wolves have litters. Five or six pups are *not* uncommon."

Sunay shuddered at the thought of birthing *that* many children at once.

Playfully, Ahmin added, "Red foxes are very much the same in that regard."

Sunay's ears flattened, and she clenched her eyes shut while chanting, "No no no no no no no... *I can't hear ya!*"

Due to that, the foxgirl wasn't watching where she was going, and in a populated street, that meant you were going to bump into someone eventually. And Sunay did just that, a very large body judging from how the foxgirl was jostled. Her eyes flew open and she immediately began to apologize before she realized who she was addressing... "Oh, Coders! I am so sor... *Kaeli?*"

Sunay didn't want to believe her eyes. She didn't want to believe her nose that told her that was Kaeli's smell. She didn't want to believe her ears when the beargirl gasped, and the voice matched as it stammered, "S... Sun... Sunay? It's... it's *you! You're alive!*"

But there was no doubting the crushing hug and the plump chest her face was buried in, and the relieved tears pent up for months finally burst. “Kaeli... it's...”

“Hush now, dearie. You're alive. We're alive. That's the best all of us could have hoped for.”

Sunay allowed her voice to lilt upwards hopefully as she tilted her head to catch Kaeli's gaze. “We?”

Kaeli smiled broadly. “You simply *must* follow me.”

The foxgirl was in a daze, trying to convince herself this wasn't some hallucination as Kaeli took a turn to the west, out of the shopping district and into the residential. The beargirl's path stopped at a three story rectangular building made from red brick and with real, honest gray shingles.

“It's nothing spectacular, but it has windows!” Kaeli giggled. “And the wee ones all have beds! Actually, we *all* have beds, come to think of it. Much better than that crumbling hole we lived in before!”

Sunay blinked, still stupefied, tripping over the “we” Kaeli mentioned earlier. She didn't dare hope that everyone made it out alive. She could *let* herself hope that and be tragically disappointed. She couldn't...

Kaeli threw open the front door and cheered, “Hey kiddies! Ol' Kaeli has a surprise for you! Gather 'round everyone!”

Sunay couldn't quite see who was stomping about inside due to her position outside the door and Kaeli's large frame blocking her view. But she could hear a lot of footprints, the mumbling of many familiar voices, and so many familiar smells. Even after months, the smells hadn't changed much.

Kaeli looked back, and rolled her eyes. “Get in here, girl! Don't make us all wait!”

Taking a deep breath, then exhaling it nervously, Sunay stepped over the threshold and Kaeli moved aside.

Everyone... was there.

Everyone she remembered from the orphanage in the woods, and two new faces she didn't recognize. They all made it.

And Sunay broke down as she was swamped by all the sounds and smells she remembered, chanting her name happily while all of her senses drowned and her eyes blurred with happy tears. Arms came from seemingly every direction in the form of hugs and welcoming pats.

“Alright, you brats!” Kaeli interjected. “Let her breathe, for Coders' sakes!”

Kaeli had successfully got the mob of chimeras to back down as Matron Miriam stomped into the landing, initially cross as she demanded, "What is the meaning of all this racket..."

The matron then quickly saw the reason, and stopped cold, one hand flying up to her mouth in surprise. Sunay cringed in anticipation, remembering the hurt that had laced Miriam's features on the fateful day they had parted ways. But when the foxgirl finally dared look the woman who had raised her in the eyes... there wasn't any hurt. Just tearful joy and relief.

Miriam nearly flung herself at Sunay, the two embracing warmly and setting off another torrent of tears. "I know you told me to yell at you later," the matron said, "but I don't think I have it in me anymore."

"Matron Miriam goin' soft? Must be all of that fancy livin' you got goin' on in here," Sunay teased.

Miriam then pushed Sunay to arms length, and gave a tight lipped, happy smile. "I will *still* correct that atrocious diction of yours, however."

"Ya won't succeed," Sunay retorted, even as her own smile betrayed any real challenge.

Kaeli then made a yelp of dismay which served to even draw attention away from the return of their prodigal daughter. "I was so excited to see Sunay again that I dropped everything I bought in town!"

There was a deep cough from the front door, and Ahmin's voice asking, "Is that where I come in?"

The massive pirate stood just outside the doorway, holding up a brown leather pack by its black drawstring. "I think you left this, ma'am."

Kaeli yelped in glee, grabbing the pack out of Ahmin's hands, then astonished at the sight of a person larger than her. "Goodness, you're a tall one, aren't you? Thanks, kind sir, we really don't have the money to pay double for food, much less for treats."

That perked up ears, at which Kaeli admonished, "You lot will get them when they're done. Now into the living room with all of you!"

Seeing Matron Miriam's scrutinizing look at the man in the door, Sunay introduced him. "This is Admiral Ahmin of the Gold Pirates. He's been my commander since we parted ways. He's also the guy who ensured the lot of your safety on the Line."

Miriam's eyebrows raised. "Is that so?"

Ahmin laughed and shook his head. "I merely went through

some contacts to figure out who would be handling you. Once I found out it was Hugo and Liona, I knew you were in good hands. They're good folk, and have put a lot of their own wealth and good standing with the Republic on the line, both figuratively and literally."

The invocation of the handlers was enough to convince Miriam that the massive pirate at least wasn't an immediate threat. "I apologize, sir, I've spent the better part of two decades wary of outsiders. It's a habit that has been hard to break."

"It's an understandable worry, I've seen it first hand in my days sailing the waters of Avalon."

At that point, Miriam really took a closer look and processed Ahmin's eyes. "I see. You're chimera too, are you?"

Sunay *knew* that, of course... but it was still something that surprised her to see voiced, as it was something her crewmates had warned her to avoid bringing up. It was indeed something he didn't encourage discussing, and that trait was evident as he curtly replied, "Yes."

Harold and Clive, two of the youngest, had been regarding Ahmin warily. The two mouseboys likely shared a father due to their similar animal traits, though not a mother as they looked nothing alike. Harold was taller with blue eyes and white splotches on his gray ears and hair; Clive was green eyed and a more solid color all around.

Harold was also the braver one of the pair, demonstrated as he was the one who finally broke from the crowd heading to the living room and standing in the presence of the shrouded and intimidating pirate. "You're... not gonna eat us, are you?"

Ahmin laughed, no doubt in an attempt to be disarming, but as he was over eight feet tall and built like a wall there wasn't really any way he could really do disarming effectively. Even when he dropped to one knee, he still loomed over the mouseboy; who was doing everything he could to keep his knees from visibly shaking.

"Mice aren't fitting prey for me, child," Ahmin said, ruffling Harold's hair playfully. "Besides, cat chimeras don't exist."

Sunay froze and tilted her head, actually thinking about it for the first time, and she honestly could not recall ever seeing or even *hearing* about a cat chimera. Tigers and panthers she had heard of, and knew of one lion on another Gold Pirate ship... but never a simple cat. She wondered why that was, until Miriam patted her on the shoulder. "Your friend has been adopted."

Harold and Clive had taken Ahmin's hands, one to each, and were leading him towards the living room. "I wouldn't worry," Sunay said. "I've seen him eat. This entire orphanage wouldn't even be worth the half-full belly it would give him."

Miriam shook her head. "Now why is it that living and working with pirates actually *improved* your grammar and diction?"

Sunay winced. "You'd be... amazed how ship life makes bein' able to speak clearly important. None of us talk great, mind, but we talk clearly."

The matron's accusing stare turned into a warm smile. "Clearly, we have much to catch up on. Come, sit with me while your commander entertains the wee ones."

That they did, taking two chairs along the perimeter of the polished pine wood floor of the living room as she looked towards the center where Ahmin crossed his legs as children eight to eighteen gathered around in awe of this giant of a man in front of them. His body nearly blocked the stone hearth fireplace entirely, casting a dim orange glow around his outline.

The foxgirl kicked off her shoes and let her toes sink into plush red carpet, and she snorted mirthfully. "Ya mean to tell me I leave and *then* ya'll get carpet?"

Miriam refused to rise to the bait. "We can afford those things when a certain foxgirl isn't devouring half our food stores at every sitting," she teased, before exhaling with content. "We've been very lucky these last months, considering how badly all those events could have spun. The citizens of Terrasa helped us restore this old storehouse and gave so generously to make it look like the home I had always dreamed of giving. Our older brats help in the town, working or serving as police and other public services..."

More happy tears crept down her face as she choked up momentarily. "This is everything I've ever wanted for the poor children who had no one else in their lives. It's not *easy*, mind. Without the generosity of others I'm not sure how we'd make it through any given season, but it's more than we've ever had before. I mean, we have beds now. Real beds with feather mattresses and pillows."

Megan stepped in front of Sunay's vision, holding a tall clear glass with orange juice. "Here, Sunay!"

The foxgirl took the glass with a thank you, nearly dropping it when the doggirl hugged her around the waist. "Oof!" Sunay grunted. "You've gotten strong."

"It's the doggie in me, Kaeli says!" Megan chirped as she pulled away. "I'm so glad you're okay! We were *so* worried for *so* long that we'd never see you again!"

"Likewise," Sunay answered. "It's nothin' short of a minor miracle that everyone got out of Avalon safely."

Megan's ears drooped fully flat, and her face fell. "Not everyone."

Sunay began going through names in her head, matching them to the faces she had seen in the new orphanage. "Oh no... Penelope?"

Miriam gave Megan a disapproving glance. "Penelope is a night guard at the city gates, Beckham is part of the city marshals, and is also not present. They return just before morning. Megan is speaking of Laron."

Sunay jerked, and her eyes darted towards the matron frantically. "What happened? What happened to Laron?"

Miriam shooed off Megan towards Ahmin's ongoing story time before turning her full attention to Sunay. "I've been trying to glean whatever information I can from merchants who pass through the region from Avalon. There hasn't been much. The only things I can say for certain is that Laron's father was executed for treason to the Republic, and that the family has not returned to Navarre."

Sunay's entire body went numb. She had learned from her history lessons and from her own travels that entire families would "disappear" on occasion, and that news *never* turned out well. They were either found buried in a shallow ditch somewhere, found near death or dead in labor camps... or never found at all.

"We don't know anything for certain," Miriam said, trying to soften the blow.

Sunay forced herself to smile. "It's alright, ma'am. I've seen and heard a lot of sad things already. One more ain't gonna break me. At least I got the good news first this time."

The foxgirl forced herself not to dwell on the sad news, instead turning her attention towards the center of the living room. At this point, Ahmin had *everyone's* attention, even Kaeli was leaning out of the doorway connecting the kitchen to the living room.

"Wow... how do you so much about the Tiger Man, mister?" Artemis asked in a cute sing-song voice that fit the nightingale that was her chimeric likeness.

Ahmin lowered his head, glancing up at Sunay momentarily, then pulling back the cowl that covered black hair striped with locks of orange, then tugging down his mask to show a broad nose and prominent cheeks dotted with tiny white whiskers.

There was a long beat of silence before the entire room erupted with glee. Ahmin hushed them, and they complied...

eventually. "You must understand, I was getting a little *too* well known, and there are many things that I do that require me to not be noticed on sight. So, this is a secret I am sharing with you... but it must remain a secret to everybody else. Can you do that for me?"

His answer was a gaggle of silent nods as he replaced his coverings. Miriam looked over at Sunay. "So all those stories were true?"

Sunay shrugged. Somehow she doubted any of them were all that true, nor were the reasons Ahmin gave for covering up his features. "Guess so."

"He's a man with a lot of inner pain, isn't he?"

The foxgirl shrugged again. "Wouldn't know. He tends to shut down any talk about himself."

"Unfortunate, as pain left to fester is like a wound that never heals."

The way Miriam said that while looking directly at Sunay with concern suggested that the matron wasn't just talking about Ahmin.

"Who wants *cookies?*" Kaeli declared, carrying a large two foot baking pan in both hands.

Not even the legendary Tiger Man of Scheherazade could match the thrill of Kaeli's almond delights. The bratlings swarmed around her waist, while the older ones formed a looser circle behind the tiny swarm of chimeric humanity. That got another genuine smile to crack Sunay's face.

Desserts were time well spent, even if by the time they were done, the sun was already setting. Even Miriam lost track of time until after the shadows had stopped being long due to there not being much of a sun to cast them. "Do you have lodging?" the matron asked. "We *do* have some spare beds... but..."

Ahmin eased Miriam's mind. "I have arrangements made. Do not waste your concerns on us."

The orphans groaned in displeasure, and Megan was outright despondent at the idea that Sunay and Ahmin were leaving. "We'll be back in the morning, children," the pirate admiral said. "We won't leave until morning of the day after. Come Sunay, I would like to sleep before the sun rises again."

Sunay didn't let partings take that much longer with the promises of a return the next day. She fell in step to the right Ahmin, content to let silence rule the walk to wherever they were going, despite Miriam's advice ringing in her head. It didn't seem right... if the admiral wanted to talk about it, he would.

"Have to admit, it felt good to take off the mask for a little while."

Sunay was so surprised to hear Ahmin speak so openly that it startled her into a stupor. As a result, her response came out awkwardly well after the fact. "Then... why don't ya? It's not like the crew would freak out over a chimera's presence."

Ahmin shook his head. "The legend of the Tiger Man of Scheherazade predates me, believe it or not. There were many such chimeras before me, due to the rituals of my origin people. In Scheherazade, whenever the previous Tiger Man passed on, the most worthy virgin in the land was presented to the Tiger God, to bear his seed and give birth to the land's chosen hero. For thousands of years, my people followed that ritual. I was the last; the whole of Scheherazade, and the Tigris continent, collapsed into the Void when I was three.

"From the moment I was born, I was burdened with expectations, and a reputation to follow, a reputation I failed before I was even old enough to read. That legend, and the memory that I had already failed it, followed me, especially among the chimeras in Avalon who were persecuted even *before* the Revolution. I was supposed to be *everywhere* at all times to save those cursed. Even when my own rage at the title and the burdens it brought boiled over, it was something that was perversely admired in story."

The towering pirate plucked his mask forward, as if he was trying to look down it. "With this... I am no longer the Tiger Man. I'm, perhaps ironically, finally allowed to be myself when I wear it."

Sunay punched him in the forearm. "Well, I never particularly liked any of those stories anyway. So yer safe wit' me!"

Ahmin laughed, his chest visibly trembling from mirth. "I shall keep that in mind."

Their path ended at an inn on the edge of town, Ahmin taking the lead as he approached the front desk. "I have a reservation for Ahmin."

The innkeeper flipped open the book at the counter, turning two pages and said, "Ah yes. The four bed room."

Sunay's left eyebrow rose. A four bed?

"That would be the one. My colleagues would have reserved it last week."

"Indeed they did. Two nights at 30 silver a piece."

Ahmin dropped a single gold piece onto the desk, and said, "Consider the rest a tip for services rendered."

"Most generous of you. Abigail will escort you to your room. Should we make note of any others who will join you?"

The pirate admiral shook his head. "That won't be necessary, thank you."

Abigail was a chimera herself, a doggirl like Megan though of a shepherd breed judging from the more prominent nose and pointed ears and dark black hair. Even after meeting so many chimeras not out of the orphanage, it was odd to see one that wasn't an orphan working at a perfectly normal job.

She was also remarkably chatty among strangers, something that orphans tended not to be by her experience. "Nice to see some chimeras from out of town. My mama was from Wynncaster, far to the north."

Ahmin played conversational. "Probably ran south during the Daynish Campaigns, didn't she? That town is actually *still* under Dayne control, if I remember rightly. Having a chimera girl probably didn't help matters."

"She figures her mother-in-law cursed her," Abigail replied. "Really didn't wanna be married anyway. Something about an arranged marriage. So she ran off with my dad when the Daynes came. I've lived here as long as I can remember. Anyway, here's your room, folks! If ya need anything, just ring the bell here!"

Abigail pointed to a large bronze bell outside the door of the room, and bowed happily before retreating back to wherever she had been before.

"Hunh. Don't hear about too many women getting cursed like that," Sunay noted once they had privacy.

Ahmin scoffed. "Why? Think the men of Avalon were the only ones with wandering eyes?"

"No. Just didn't hear about it too much."

The admiral laughed at Sunay's defensive reply as he opened the door to the room, and ducked under the header to enter. "It was easier to blame the man for most infidelity, as it was more socially acceptable, which of course led to noblemen talking more freely about their infidelity as a badge of honor, which made it easier to blame them for infidelity. Welcome to the vicious circle of Avalon noble customs... which were often anything but noble."

It was at that point that Sunay learned why Ahmin requested four beds. He left one for Sunay, then pushed the other three together and laid down diagonally across the result. He still didn't fit exactly, he had to bend his knees in a way that couldn't have been completely comfortable, but a lot better than trying to fold himself onto a single bed.

Sunay herself splayed out on her bed. "Then ya must be looking forward to being away from all that then."

Ahmin grunted in indifference. "Not really. Aramathea is a mess of bureaucracy that treats *all* foreigners equally... equally terribly. You could live there a hundred years and still not have the same legal respect as a babe that was born that day in Grand Aramathea. It's a land that cares little about what you know, and everything about *who* you know.

"Reaht is a militaristic dictatorship that considers their emperor to be the mouthpiece of the Coders. There's true equality in that country, if by equality you mean just as likely as any citizen to die because the emperor doesn't like your hat that day or get thrown to your death in any one of the roughly ten thousand campaigns of expansion they partake in every year."

"What about the Free Provinces?" she asked.

"Not fond of the barely controlled anarchy. Fall to sleep in a town and wake up the next morning to see it all burning because a larger city-state decided your town was a blight that had to be removed. Even in relatively peaceful provinces like this, you're entirely at the mercy of larger powers that may or not decide you have what they want, and can take it without consequence."

Sunay giggled. "Well, that explains why ya spend yer time on the open seas."

"It's not because I like the tight fit of sea life," He said ruefully. "Out there, I'm free... I don't have to be anyone's hero... I can just be myself."

He quickly shifted topics abruptly. "So, since we're both in such a sharing mood, care to tell me what the matron said that had you all down before you started pretending to be all happy?"

The foxgirl took and released a deep breath. She supposed it *was* fair. "There was... a boy named Laron... that I knew in Navarre. His father was a former lord of the town, and sided with the rebels. He and I... I guess we were in love, I think. It was only a few months."

"Sometimes a few months is all it can take for strong affection to form," Ahmin said.

"Maybe. Maybe not. But I liked him, and he liked me at the very least. During all the mess that led me to your camp, his family was being rounded up and taken to Snake River."

Ahmin nodded. "That explains Cavalier Norman's presence.

The Dog of the Republic was investigating nobles who might still be harboring Royalist ties, and learned through some means that a girl matching one of Morgana's chimeras was at the orphanage. The chances that you were a bastard child of King George was high enough that he went on a fox hunt."

"But how would he know that, though? The only person outside of the town who knew I even existed was..."

Ahmin interrupted before her theory could wander. "I suspect Lord Lavin had chimeras of his own at the orphanage, and was supplying monetary aid. He would want to know exactly what, where, and even *who* he was giving money to. In investigating something else, Norman either came upon records of the orphanage, or Lavin offered it willingly to try and blunt the Republic's judgment of some *other* crime he committed."

That would explain Laron's warning, at the very least, that his father had ratted out the orphanage and why Norman would have been looking for her specifically. "Do you think I'm some bastard daughter of the king?" She asked, "Would that explain why that Cavalier was hunting me?"

"It would. At this point, the disapproval of the Parliament is so high that the people, and most certainly the remaining nobility would quite likely embrace an illegitimate child of King George. As for the question of whether *you* are such a child, I'm afraid there's no way of knowing. The king was *hardly* the only noble Morgana was paid to curse, and as she herself claimed, she was hardly the only one who used the red fox."

He looked at her with narrowing eyes. "Why does it matter anyway?"

"It doesn't," Sunay answered. "Things were just so crazy that day that it's nice to kinda figure out why they happened. Anyway, Laron's father's appeal apparently didn't work. He was executed."

"And the rest of his family disappeared," Ahmin finished, his eyes closing in sympathy. "That is unfortunately far too common. If you wish, I can send an appeal for information for this Laron fellow. But considering the Administrator in charge, pfeh. I'll just do it. But... that... will have to be when we get back... to the ship. Laron was the name, you said?"

Ahmin yawned, then apologized as he rolled onto his back and closed his eyes again. "Sorry. I must seem terribly callous."

"Nah. Get some sleep."

Sunay watched the rise and fall of his chest as it quickly

slowed down. Ahmin had been tired, it would seem. It didn't terribly surprise her, she can't remember one time that she had caught him sleeping or waking up. It was astonishing when she thought about it; the degree that her admiral kept his distance from everyone around him.

"Well, ya may not like the idea... but yer a hero to me, at any rate," she whispered before she curled up into a ball and fell asleep herself.

# Chapter Eight: Fox and Wolf

Kaeli insisted that Sunay spend some time with her after breakfast, while the rest of the children were being tutored. Miriam had little problem with that, fearing that Sunay would have been a distraction anyway, both with her presence and her 'sinful butchering of proper language.' Sunay had little problem with it either, especially when she saw that lessons in the new orphanage were even more orderly and disciplined than the ones that she bristled against.

"I can't imagine having four lessons all in a row without a break. And with four different teachers at that!" she exclaimed.

"Definitely different from when I was a wee one, that's for sure," Kaeli agreed. "Back then, you had one tutor that taught you alone, provided you had the money and influence to afford it. Bur this way is better, I think, at least for those who don't have all the money that can be spent. The bratlings are going to learn more than a trade, they're learning to think and *improve* on whatever path they take in life."

Sunay shrugged. "Guess so."

"Speaking of paths in life... you *must* tell me where your adventures have taken *you.*"

Sunay didn't think it was all that much, until she started explaining her travels across the seas of Avalon, and all the port towns and island cities the crew sailed by or docked at. From Far West Wharf, the secluded fishing village on a rocky island that as its named implied was the most western habitable land in all the continent, to the Salt Cliffs of Pershing's Port, they were places Kaeli had never known of, or at best only heard of in tales from others.

And then the beargirl's eyes lit up with wonder when Sunay mentioned Tortuga. "You've been to *Tortuga?* I would hear so many stories about that place when I was a girl! What was it like?"

Sunay *really* didn't want to have this discussion. Those memories *still* kinda made her entire body shiver. "Well it was... colorful. Although I was there in the winter, so there wasn' much going on. Just a lot of snow and ice. Domina Morgana had kicked everyone out of her tower too, so there wasn' even much to see *there.*"

"You saw the Domina? Stories say that she has so much magical power that she doesn't even age. Is that true?"

Sunay wanted to talk about Morgana even *less*. "I dunno. She looked awfully young, even though there's no way she could be."

"You *met* her? In person?"

The foxgirl could no longer hold back the shivers. "Y... yes."

"What was she like? I've heard so many tales about her that say so many different things that I don't know truth from fiction."

Sunay cringed, her ears flat and her tail fluffing from the memory. "Creeeeeeeeeeeeeepy..." she finally said with a slow groan.

"Oh, that's just because Domina Morgana has been so invested in her research that she rarely interacts with anyone," interjected Rola from the doorway.

Sunay's ears couldn't have lowered any further, which was about the only reason why the foxgirl didn't look more unnerved when they both she and Kaeli turned to the sound of Rola's voice.

The wolf spirit looked bright and happy as ever, with a knowing, playful smirk that showed off a hint of the woman's left canines. "When I was in that city many years ago, there weren't many she allowed in her tower to begin with. Just her and her apprentice, with *maybe* two or three servants to fetch whatever thing the Domina desired. I'm not sure she even *knows* how to interact with other humans anymore."

"Rola!" Kaeli said amiably. "I didn't know you were in town!"

Sunay pointed between the two, and demanded to the beargirl, "Wait. You *know* her?"

"Oh yes!" Kaeli answered. "She and her husband are some of the most kind providers to the orphanage. I don't know how she makes any money selling stuff to us!"

"We make enough," Rola answered cryptically. "Though nothing for your little ones this time through, which was why we didn't stop in. Law and I will be heading back to Beredon, then towards the Gold Coast to get some of the spring crop from Aramathea. By our next visit, we should have so many wonderful exotic foods for you to play with."

Kaeli clapped in delight. "I so love experimenting!"

"And good day to you, little fox," Rola finally said, giving Sunay a broad, tooth-filled grin.

"Hi," Sunay replied quickly, wanting to slink away to anywhere else as soon as possible.

Kaeli noticed the reaction, and clicked her tongue disapprovingly at the foxgirl. "What are you all skittish for? Rola's good folk!"

Rola's grin never wavered. "Wolves are known to eat foxes when they're hungry. It's a sad truth."

"Well, nice little Rola here isn't gonna eat you or anyone, Sunay. She's harmless!"

The wolf spirit's grin broadened beyond what Sunay thought was natural. "Yes. Harmless."

Sunay sincerely doubted that in every way possible.

Rola pointed flippantly between the two. "So, the two of you know each other as well?"

"Sunay here was one of our orphanage while it was still in Avalon. We had no idea she was even still *alive* before yesterday," Kaeli said, throwing her right arm around the foxgirl's shoulders amiably.

Rola clapped her hands once, and chirped with glee. "Then these have been pleasant days for *both* of you! They simply *must* be celebrated! Come with me!"

"Do we have to?" Sunay asked meekly.

Rola grabbed both by the hands, and started leading them away with far more strength than her small frame should have possessed. "Yes. You have to," She said in a tone that did not encourage further debate, out of the shopping district and towards the town square.

Her destination was another blocky red brick building directly on the eastern edge of the square. With two distinct stories, Sunay initially assumed it was an inn, until she saw the letters engraved in a gray stone block above a pair of thick oak doors stained to near black: "Hall of the Forlorn Knights."

"It's a drinking hall," Rola explained when she saw Sunay's confusion. "If you've been the northern parts of Avalon, I can't believe you haven't seen one. They're inspired by Daynish mead halls, no doubt, although to find one this far south I'm sure is peculiar."

"I've seen this place before, of course, but never went inside," Kaeli said. "What's it like?"

Rola pushed open the left side door, and grinned saucily. "Like every tavern you've ever seen, only more. Come!"

The entry was remarkably plain, by Sunay's estimation, tan carpet and darkly stained oak with a row of empty coat racks and hooks, most likely left from the winter months.

A mostly bald man in his fifties and a violet suit with gold buttons held position in front of the door on the other side of the entry, and bowed in recognition as the wolf spirit stepped forward. "Ah,

Madam Rola, it is a pleasure to see you here," he said. "It's been since fall, I do believe."

"Indeed it has, Oswalt," Rola replied. "I seek a single table room if there is one available for me and my guests."

"Of course. Step inside, Patton will guide you."

The man stepped to the left, pushing open the door in the process and allowing the three inside. Sunay's eyes ran along the entire hall the moment she entered, surprised by the sight. It certainly wasn't like any tavern she had seen, Rola was right about that. What looked like a two story building was actually one story with a second balcony level that ran along the perimeter, with individual rooms along the outside on both levels. The central hall was marked by three rows of wooden tables, though mostly unoccupied at the moment.

Patton was the opposite of Oswalt in every way Sunay could see. Where Oswalt was short, pudgy, and bald, Patton was so lanky that she wondered if there was any meat on his tall frame, and had a full head of silver hair. "Madam Rola. come this way. There is a corner room for you on the second floor."

"You need a membership to enter this hall," Rola said after they had fallen in step behind Patton. "This central chamber is for the actual Forlorn Knights, deposed cavaliers who escaped the Avalon Revolution and didn't want to seek refuge in Tortuga. We *could* celebrate here, but it's so very public and I find being in the open when I drink terribly distasteful."

"Membership here can't be cheap..." Kaeli gasped in wonder.

"It's not, normally," Rosa said, looking over her shoulder to flash another unnerving grin that made Sunay shiver, "but I can be a very persuasive woman."

Finally something Rola said that Sunay had little doubt of its authenticity.

The stairs to the second floor were on the south side of the hall, requiring the group to cross nearly the entire length of the chamber to reach them. On the way, they caught the eyes of many of the denizens, only to see every single one of them *avert* said gazes when they saw Rola leading the procession.

"They respect me," Rola said, tilting her head in the direction of the population in the hall.

Sunay suspected Rola saw very little difference, if any, between respect and fear.

The steps weren't particularly elaborate, but stained dark and with a well polished brass handrail that matched the railing on the second floor balcony. There was also green felt carpet on the second floor unlike the bare wood of the main hall, along with currently extinguished candles along the walls. There were ten doors that Sunay could count, each with a brass bell mounted just outside.

Patton led the three women to the southwest corner and opened the door on the west side. "And here you are, ladies. May I get your first round?"

"The house special, please," Rola said.

"As you wish. I shall return. Do be seated."

The room itself was fairly spacious, with enough room for a 6 foot circular oak table with matching chairs and a white tablecloth. Rola took the chair with her back to the window, and beckoned; "Well, come on in!"

Sunay and Kaeli took chairs opposite Rola, and for a very awkward period, none of them spoke, which managed to unnerve Sunay even *more* than when the wolf would talk. That silence ruled the room until Patton returned with a tray bearing three large clear glass mugs filled with a pale yellow liquid with a small foamy head.

"And here are your drinks, ladies. Please ring the bell if you need anything else."

"We will, Patton," Rola acknowledged, and said nothing further until the attendant had left and closed the door behind him. "Ah! This place has a wonderful hard lemonade! Just be careful, because it does have a bit of a kick!"

That the wolf downed half of her mug without taking a breath suggested otherwise, until Sunay took a sip and recoiled. It really wasn't *that* strong, but the burn surprised her. She had lemonade before, and had been expecting something else, like what she had... back in Navarre... with...

"Alright, so what's got you all melancholy all of a sudden? You weren't like this on the road here," Rola asked. "And don't tell me it's because you're scared I'm going to eat you."

Sunay *really* didn't want to discuss it, especially to someone like the wolf spirit... But Kaeli did anyway. "She had a boyfriend in Avalon, the city of Navarre, whose family was taken by the Republican Police."

"Oh," Rola replied, and her concern sounded genuine.

"The boy's father was executed, and no one's heard about his family. Matron Miriam tries to get news wherever she can, but the people who come through don't know much."

"Well, of course not," Rola agreed. "Those that come through

Terrasa usually take the Southern roads and up north along the coast of the Western Forever Sea. If the family was taken to the courts in Snake River, very little news would drift south like that. Snake River is closer to the Free Provinces and the Northern Great Trade Line than any of the coastal towns."

"My admiral is gonna look into it," Sunay grumbled, even as she felt her vision blurring from the drink she was nursing. How much alcohol was *in* this thing?

"Doesn't mean I can't," Rola insisted. "I know exactly who to talk to and what questions to ask. Rest assured, there are few things the merchant's guild *doesn't* see if you ask the right people with the right... incentives. I could probably have news by fall if everything went right. There's even a Guild Hall in Beredon, just go in, give the bookkeeper your name and ask if you have any messages from Law and Rola."

"I'm gonna be in Aramathea for Coders' knows how long. Might not be comin' back this way for years."

Rola shrugged indifferently. "There's a Merchant's Guild in damn near every coastal town in the southern empire too. I'll just send it to the Guild Hall in Grand Aramathea. It'll get there just as easily."

Sunay couldn't fight back the distrust. "Why are you helpin' me?"

"Because when I was trying to get back home, there was a period where I had a terrible fight with Law, and... we parted ways. Despite our argument, I spent the better part of a month worried sick about him. I remember that feeling of not knowing. I know how terrible it is. If I can help someone else find *something* resembling ease of mind or at the very least closure, why shouldn't I if it won't be any trouble at all?"

Sunay's ears drooped, and Rola reached over to pat the foxgirl's shoulder. "You poor thing. I honestly was only teasing you with all my scary little posturing. You're a good, sweet girl... makes me wonder how you're a pirate at all."

"*Gold* Pirate," Sunay asserted, fighting her tongue to move properly, with moderate success. "We're a differ...en breed."

"Ah, well *that* explains it," Rola said with a wink. "The Gold Pirates are everywhere. You never really know who could be counted among them, on land or sea."

Even with a mind tipsy from alcohol, Sunay caught the hint. "What are ya imp... implee... sayin'?"

"That you never really know, and sometimes you *can't* know. You know?"

That answer was less than worthless. "No."

"Good."

Sunay had to be getting drunk. Because otherwise this conversation wouldn't make any sense.

"So, who is ready for another round?" Rola asked, as she slapped her empty mug down onto the table, then stood up to ring the bell for service. "I think I know just what we need... something with a little more zest to it."

Another round might just be what Sunay needed, really. If anything it would make the silly words stop.

~ ~ ~ ~ ~

"And so *then* he says, 'She's no fox. She's a *wolf.* And she's my *wife!'"*

Sunay's brain felt like it was being stirred around in her skull, being startled to whatever excuse for alertness this was by Kaeli and Rola's boisterous laughter.

"Oh goodness! He didn't get the metaphor, eh?" Kaeli chortled, her voice slightly slurred from the drink she had imbibed.

What happened? Sunay remembered getting another round of... whatever that drink was. She knew it was strong, but had the second drink really been enough to knock her out? Had there been a third? There *might* have been a third. She vaguely remembered *something* about a third. Maybe?

"Law can be dreadfully simple for someone so smart," Rola confirmed, her voice not affected but with a good rosy color to her normally pale cheeks. "Oh! The lightweight's awake!"

Sunay tried to turn her head to figure out which of the three Rolas was speaking, and to whom, but trying to do so made her vision spin worse. "Huh?" the foxgirl finally said, which at the moment was about the extent her lips would cooperate with her head.

Rola clicked her tongue and teased, "And you call yourself a pirate? Shameful!"

"Ah... Ahmin duddn't has us... drinkin'... on da sherp," Sunay tried to say, but wasn't even certain that what came out of her mouth was even *that* coherent. "End I don do much when we on leaves. Avalawn dunt like peep mah age drinkin' too muh."

"Well, *that's* going to have to change!" Rola teased. "When we meet again, I expect you to hold your liquor!"

Sunay would have agreed to about anything if it stopped Rola from yelling. "Shure."

"Good. Because while it was adorable seeing you drunk, I'd rather not have you offer to groom my tail until *I* am suitably inebriated as well."

The foxgirl went pale. Had she done that?

Kaeli chortled. "You *did!* Rola went white as a ghost! You then straight passed out right on the table not even a moment later. We had a good laugh about that one."

Sunay whimpered, and her ears went flat.

Rola patted her on the head. "Oh, I was flattered that you found my tail so pretty. I do take very good care of it. I'd recommend you do the same, you could have such a lovely, plush tail if you'd take care of it right."

Sunay really was too drunk to put up with being insulted about her tail. She thought she *did* maintain it well.

Rola smiled. "Not that it isn't quite nice already, but with the right soap... you can't just use the same stuff as on your head. Tail fur is thinner and more densely packed. You need a gentle shampoo that can get deep to the root. I can grab you some before you leave tomorrow. You'll love it!"

Coders, *anything* to get the wolf to shut up. "Shure." She then looked out the window and noticed that it was rapidly approaching evening. "Pits, how long was I out?"

Kaeli paused to think, then said, "A few hours at least. I was getting rather worried, but Rola kept checking you out and saying you were all right, just napping."

Sunay rubbed her forehead and groaned. "That explains the start of this hangover."

Kaeli slapped her forehead. "And I need to get back to the orphanage to get dinner started. I hope you can at least fake being sober, Sunay, because the matron would have my hide if you stumbled in half dead."

Sunay slapped her cheeks and exhaled with a puttering of her lips. She focused on the empty mug in front of her, trying to anchor her vision. It worked somewhat, even if she had to talk slower than usual. "Yeah. If anyone asks, I'll just tell them I'm feeling a little under the weather. Probably wouldn't fool Matron Miriam, but everyone else would buy it, I'm sure."

In reality, Sunay only had opportunity to get back to the orphanage and say farewell, because Ahmin didn't give her opportunity for much else.

"Rola and Law are leaving for Beredon tomorrow morning, and have already offered us use of their cart," he explained. "Just because the Gold Pirates aren't poor doesn't mean we shouldn't try and be frugal. And I think you need your rest, you look a little ill."

Ahmin carried that ruse until they were out of earshot of the orphanage, on their way back to the inn. "I sincerely hope you'll have sobered up by the time we return to the ship. I'd hate to have to put you in the brig for a week."

Sunay groaned weakly, and whimpered, "It was... whatever that stuff Rola had us drink. Wiped me clean, I tell ya."

After a beat, the foxgirl then asked, "Are Rola and Law Gold Pirates?"

"It's possible," Ahmin admitted. "Those of us who work on land generally have to be quieter about their status than we do. I couldn't tell you conclusively if one or either of them are, as I don't have that authority. But it *is* true that merchants are often recruited as operatives, as they have the freedoms necessary to move about and share information easier than other civilian professions."

"I dunno why that's such a big deal," Sunay said. "Aren't we pretty much immune from prosecution?"

Ahmin glared at her. "That's not something we like to invoke terribly often. The political entities that *give* us that protection put themselves at risk if they have to grant it too often, nor does it help us much in areas like the Free Provinces and the Daynelands, where our reach is more limited.

"People of this continent need to *think* that nothing is amiss. Any random citizen wandering about sniffing around sensitive areas where they don't belong would cause no amount of problems that not even the political entities at our disposal could easily fix, if they could fix it at all.

"But what I can tell you is that there *are* a lot of us about. We have many duties, as you know. It's difficult to maintain the balance of powers in this continent so that we don't have another World War, and with the Void on all sides, this remaining continent can ill afford such a large scale conflict."

Sunay knew the Gold Pirates were a massive organization, but at the same time, the picture she had formed in her head hadn't reflected that reality. That she was a part of something so far reaching that you could cross paths with one of your ilk and never even know it unless they said something about it was something she hadn't even considered.

"How many of us are out there? I mean, roughly?"

Ahmin shrugged his shoulders. “I don't get a population count. All I know is the fleet, which numbers three hundred ships of various sizes and fifty thousand men and women. Operations on land involve more people, I'm sure, but aren't as coordinated. It's a big world, even now, Sunay. We need a big operation to handle it all.”

She remained silent, even as they returned to the inn and settled into their rooms. As Ahmin dropped down onto his makeshift triple-bed, she finally asked, “So, on to Aramathea then, eh?”

“Yes. I will receive a briefing from my captains in the empire shortly upon arrival in imperial waters. Hopefully, I won't have a chimera running for her life right into the camp this time.”

That got Sunay to chuckle. “Why would that be such a bad thing?”

“Because we can't afford the amount of food *two* of you would eat.”

“Funny man,” Sunay said with a sneer. “You're just so funny I forget how funny you are.”

“Get some sleep, Sunay,” Ahmin ordered. “You aren't yourself when you're hung over.”

# Chapter Nine: Socrato's Death Ray

Admiral Ahmin met his captains shortly after crossing into the authority of The Imperial Aramathea, and they swiftly made their way east, though the admiral didn't explain why initially, only ordering them to full sail towards the eastern port of Troja.

Sunay watched forlornly as they passed the diamond glittered cliffs on which Grand Aramathea stood, even though she knew there was no chance any word from Rola would be already waiting. She focused on her work, if only because whatever had gotten Ahmin in such a rush, it had to be significant enough to stir haste in the pirate admiral.

That was *no* easy task.

At least the sights were pretty. Aramathea had *that* much going for it at the very least, it was a very beautiful part of the continent with a great variety of fertile plains, picturesque cliffs, sandy beaches, inlets and coves.

Although the forests left much to be desired as far as she could see. The trees were dismal, bushy things barely more than bushes, nothing like the thick-trunked oak and maple trees in the south of Avalon, much less the mighty evergreens found in the northern part of the Republic. It was disappointing.

By the time they got to the eastern side of the empire, the landscape had become barren, dry and arid.

The Denali Desert, Ahmin had called it, some of the most inhospitable lands on the continent outside of the Icy Expanse far north of even the Daynelands. There weren't even the cactus plants that she had heard of. There wasn't even *sand.*

It was just a dry desolate rocky waste, and Aramathea's interest in it was simply because of what was *underneath* it: mines of coal, silver, gold, and black oil. This was why the town of Troja was founded on one of the few coastal areas suitable for a dock, with fresh water nearby from an underground river.

"We won't be here for long," Ahmin declared. "Don't even drop anchor. We are picking up one person, then going right back out to sea. I shall return shortly."

The *Goldbeard* was famous for not having much turnover in crew, members even eschewing opportunities on other ships to remain under Ahmin's command. Sunay had been the first addition in nearly two years. This would make two such additions in less than half that time. A cursory glance at her crew-mates told her that fact had *not* been missed by those on the deck.

"We're not lackin' for anythin', are we?" Sunay asked. Ahmin had her working with the crew duty list under Jacques's supervision over the last few weeks. "Who could we be addin'?"

"Don't rightly know," Jacques said. "He hasn't told me anything either. I can only guess it's some sort of specialist for whatever this mission is."

And it would also explain why the admiral had been mum about the whole deal. Ahmin didn't like having to explain everything twice. He'd wait until he had all the people gathered and have one briefing. Of course, that led to discussion about what sort of specialist they were getting... as they couldn't think of what could be needed that the crew couldn't already handle.

Their answer would finally come within the hour, as Ahmin returned with a much smaller man in a desert robe in tow. Upon boarding, he cast aside the large draping garment, to reveal a middle-aged head of brown hair streaked with gray, and garb suitable for the heat, a loose white shirt with elbow length sleeves, and light brown knee-length trousers cinched at the waist by a white leather belt.

But what immediately caught everyone else's attention was the satchel slung over his shoulder, with two red leather-bound books sticking out of the top. Not even scholars like Joffe carried their books around.

This man was a mage.

"Marco," he said simply. "It's a pleasure to be working with you."

Ahmin didn't allow for pleasantries. "Jacques, go down to the row deck and grab Gurgn. Then you join Marco, Joffe, Sunay, Juno and myself in my cabin."

Sunay's eyebrows rose. She was going to be part of the briefing? That was a surprise.

The admiral beckoned his designated crew to follow him, Jacques continuing down the stairs after the rest broke off below decks towards Ahmin's cabin. The massive pirate set up maps and other documents and schematics while Jacques arrived with the rowmaster.

"Gurgn, I trust the crew has remained drilled in combat?" the admiral asked.

"Aye," Gurgn answered. "They're as ready to cross blades as

they ever were, even the little fox here."

Sunay's eyes narrowed at the use of the pet name. She was sixteen at this point, and more than the physical equal of damn near everyone on the crew. How much longer was she going to be the greenhorn?

"Good," Ahmin said with a nod. "I know it's been a while for this crew, but we're needed for a raid, and this crew is the only one I am comfortable with doing it discreetly."

Sunay trembled eagerly at the thought. She knew the Gold Pirates would occasionally live up to the title, even though the *Goldbeard's* crew hadn't done so since she came aboard. But where regular pirates raided for food, supplies, and wealth, the Gold Pirates had political or military reasons to do so... and she doubted this raid would be any different.

The first focus of attention was Ahmin pointing to the sea chart, where he drew a black circle with a charcoal marker. From their current position it was about two days travel out to sea. "This is Sacili, pretty much a hunk of volcanic rock sticking out of the ocean maybe a mile and a half wide at best. The Aramatheans have set up a military outpost here on this island, where they are constructing a weapon they think could allow them long-range attack capabilities on Reahtan interests."

From there, he revealed the blueprints for something that Sunay couldn't make heads or tails of, but that was why Joffe was there. The engineer snatched up the designs hurriedly, and his eyes danced while he flipped through each of the five pages. "This... is Socrato's Death Ray."

Jacques's eyebrows cocked in curiosity. "Socrato... isn't he...?"

Ahmin confirmed, "The Dominus of Kartage, yes. The same man. Don't let his peaceful and altruistic reputation now fool you. Back in his younger days, he was a man desperate to prove his worth to the empire, and his list of potential crimes in his pursuit of power are... lengthy, to say the least. His additions to the Aramathean war machine allowed his empire to annex part of Sparia for the first time in nearly two centuries. He's been on our watch list for some time... even if our agents in Kartage tell us he's focused on more productive things now."

Joffe hadn't even looked up. "Many of his inventions were practical, like the ballista. Some were more situational, but still useful. Then... there is this. The Death Ray. In theory, it would be the most powerful weapon known to man, harnessing the power of the sun, focusing it into a single point, and unleashing a beam of intense heat that could theoretically hit targets miles away."

Sunay tilted her head, trying to process the concept. "Would that even *work?*"

"In theory? Yes. In practicality? Not terribly. There were so many factors that were required before the theory could even manifest. If there were any clouds in the sky, the weapon didn't have enough sunlight. And with the way the sun moved in the sky, it required constant adjustment of the mirrors. A mage could handle those details, but Socrato was trying to design something that didn't require use of a mage, as magic users are very rare."

Joffe dropped the designs back on the desk, pointing at it. "Someone's modified Socrato's old blueprints. They've got all the mirrors and the weapon itself on a rotating mechanism that's linked together to automatically take sun position into account as the day goes on. This is what I want you to see, Sir Marco."

"Just Marco. I'm Free Province born, raised, and trained," the mage corrected. "But yes, I see what you're pointing at. Whoever redesigned this did away with Socrato's limitations. It's using a mage and a focusing crystal."

"An' what does that do?" Sunay asked.

"A focusing crystal is something mages use to focus their powers they are channeling, hence the name. For very complex magical arts, a focusing crystal is vital in order to handle the tremendous amounts of energy being released. In this case, a strong enough mage with a large enough crystal could not only clear the skies to make sure the weapon has enough sun, he or she could alter the path of the beam itself, rather than it traveling in a straight line."

Marco's voice grew grim as he explained the possibilities. "As long as the weapon was in the sun, the mage in charge could fire it in practically any direction, as well as bend the beam along the curvature of the planet. Aramathea could theoretically hit any target in the world from this location as long as the mage knew what obstructions were in the way."

Ahmin added in summary, "Obviously, such a weapon, if it were to reach functionality, would completely disrupt the balance of power on the continent. Our job is to neutralize it before it comes to fruition. This will require three elements to be successful."

The admiral then unrolled a map of the island itself, with points of interest already marked. He pointed to Marco, and said, "You are needed first to give us the illusion of an Aramathean ship. That will allow us to approach the site without too much trouble. After that, you will go with Sunay when we make landfall. The two of you will assault the weapon directly, do whatever it takes to destroy the thing. It is possible that the mage or mages that will use the thing is already on site, so be ready for that."

"Easiest way to do that would be to destroy the focusing crystal," Marco said. "There's a reason why Socrato was trying to design this weapon without using one. Such crystals are quite rare, and at the size this weapon would need are also quite fragile."

Ahmin then pointed to a building on the island's north side. "Juno, you will be responsible for eliminating Callast, the engineer that redesigned the weapon. Our intelligence puts him most likely at this cabin, as well as any designs he may have on site. Other agents have already taken care of designs on record in Grand Aramathea, these should be all that are left."

Then he met eyes with Jacques and Gurgn. "We and the rest of the strike team will be providing a distraction for those three. We will land first, and attack the south side of the island. We have no established goal, we just want to draw as many Aramatheans in for as long as we can hold them."

Marco then spoke again, reaching into his satchel and pulling out three tiny while pearls, handing one to Juno, Ahmin, and Sunay. "And I suppose that is where these come in. These are telepathy stones, they simulate the mental communication that mages can use to contact other mages at long distances. Use these to help coordinate our movements and extraction once the mission is complete."

Sunay held it up to her right eye, noticing how the pearl white color was actually shifting and moving. She wasn't entirely fond of magic after her experience in Tortuga, and wasn't particularly thrilled about this either. "How does it work?" she asked, more out of suspicion than curiosity.

"Just put in your ear, think about who you're trying to speak to, and talk normally. If the person you are trying to communicate with is either a mage or has a similar stone, they'll hear you."

The foxgirl *still* didn't like it, but suspected nothing anyone could say would change her opinion on that score. Reluctantly, she put the object into her right ear. It fit surprisingly snugly, so well in fact that her first fear was that she wouldn't be able to get it out. Putting her mind on Ahmin, she said, "Hello? Can ya hear me?"

"Yes," Ahmin answered. "But that would be true anyway as I'm roughly eight feet from you."

She heard an echo of Ahmin's voice in her head that matched his words, which she guessed was the telepathic stone doing its work just a hint slower than normal speech. Sunay sighed heavily in resignation; as long as someone was able to pull it out of her head once this was all over she'd be able to cope.

"The distraction team will disembark first on the south side of the island, then the *Goldbeard* will swing to the east, where Juno will disembark. Finally, Sunay and Marco will disembark on the north side. After that, it will loop around the island and extract us in that same order. Bear in mind, there *is* the possibility that your rowboats will be seized or otherwise unable to sail. You *may* have to swim. It's happened before, right Jacques?"

The first mate bit his lower lip guiltily, and offered a sheepish smile. "Yeah, it's happened before. If you hesitate or panic, there's the chance you won't be able to be extracted. That can be bad news."

Ahmin finished the briefing with his final orders. "Once we are all aboard, Marco, you will need to conjure an invisibility illusion, that should allow us a fairly easy escape and to shake off pursuit. Jacques, head to the deck, give Bolin a heading of two hundred and sixty-six degrees at full sail. The rest of you return to your assigned posts. If all goes according to plan, we launch the raid at first light in two days. Dismissed."

Juno caught Sunay barely a step past the cabin door. "Wow, first big mission for ya, and you've got an important job too!" the spidergirl said.

"Not the first for you I take it?" Sunay replied.

"Nope! I've been on a couple over the years. I'm usually the assassin type like this time, because ya know I'm good at climbing into seemingly impossible places and I can generate a venom in my fangs that can kill with one good chomp. But ya know that."

"And it doesn't bother ya?"

The spidergirl shrugged. "I mean, in a way, it's what I was born to do. This is the sort of thing we do, Sunay. Sometimes it puts us at odds with people. And sometimes, when yer at odds with people, deadly violence is the result."

Juno patted Sunay on the shoulder playfully as the spidergirl dashed ahead towards the stairs. "Don't worry!" she called back. "The admiral wouldn't have given you the job if he didn't trust ya to do it!"

That *wasn't* what Sunay was worried about, but if Juno didn't have a problem with her role, then Sunay really had no business butting in.

"She's right, you know."

Sunay nearly jumped, and she spun about. Marco could move pretty quietly... unless he was using magic or something.

"*You* ever been involved in a raid?"

Marco shook his head. "Not something like this. I was a mercenary fighting for city-states in the Free Provinces during the last Daynish Campaign, though. I remember my first time in a fight, and it was pretty damn scary. Do you trust the people around you to have prepared you properly?"

"Of course I do!"

"Then there shouldn't be a problem."

Sunay rolled her eyes. "There ain't a problem. I'm fine!"

"Then why do you seem lost in thought?"

"Because I really don't like swabbin' the deck, and I'm takin' my sweet time getting' back up there," she said, then added, "I'm sure I'll be a big ol' bundle o' nerves by go time. But for now, I'm fine. Save the pep talks for then, 'kay?"

Marco nodded in acknowledgment, stepping around Sunay to go further down the stairs, where she guessed his cabin was. She doubted he'd be sleeping on a cot. Lucky bastard. Sunay, meanwhile, returned to the deck and with a forlorn sigh grabbed her mop and started swabbing.

Sure, she could die in a raid, but she could also die being swept overboard by rough seas. At least fighting had be more engaging than *this*.

~ ~ ~ ~ ~

Sacili was pretty much exactly as Ahmin described it, a hunk of black rock sticking out of the ocean with nothing notable on its own merits. It wasn't even jagged like most volcanic rock had a tendency to be; ages of weathering polishing the surface into a smooth domed shape up to the center of the tiny island where the Death Ray was installed.

"Seems we got here just in time," Ahmin noted, handing his telescopic lens to Jacques for the first mate to take a look. "It looks damn near completion to me."

Jacques gave a look himself, and beckoned Sunay over. "Get a look at this, little fox."

Sunay momentarily blinked in confusion, wondering why he would be calling for her, but nonetheless obeyed, taking the lens and putting it up to her right eye.

Her first observation was that the designs didn't do the scale of the machine justice. It had to be at least two hundred feet from edge to edge of the mirror array, some of them reflecting light back into the lens and forcing her to squint her eye in order to keep looking.

The rest of the machination wasn't nearly as eye-catching, a bunch of gears and shimmering steel with an ivory pedestal in front. On that pedestal a blood red crystal, tiny in comparison to everything else, sat on a golden stand. That was the focusing crystal, she guessed.

"That's what you and Marco have to somehow demolish," Jacques said into her ear. "I don't envy you that. It looks pretty heavily guarded."

The statement prompted Sunay to tilt the telescope down, where she did indeed see a score of Aramathean soldiers, their bronze-plated armor gleaming, and a wooden cabin which quite likely held more. "Well, isn't that what yer supposed to try and help with?" she asked.

The first mate nodded slightly. "That's true. Let's hope we can do that."

Ahmin's voice interrupted the conversation. "Marco, I trust the illusion is active?"

The mage had been leaning back against the main mast with his eyes closed. Had one of his books not been open in front of him, and his hand hovering over said book and pale blue wisps of energy hovering inches off the page, Sunay would have thought he was asleep.

In one abrupt motion, he pulled his hand away, slapped the book shut, and opened his eyes. "It is. It was difficult reaching out to so many minds, but they are inherently inclined to believe that only one of their ships would dare approach anyway. I can't promise the illusion will hold once we start attacking and they put the hints together, but it will serve us at least that far."

"It will have to do," Ahmin said with pursed lips. "Assault team, get to the boats!"

Gurgn and nine other men of the rowing team comprised the bulk of that unit, joined by Ahmin and Jacques as they filtered into three of the rowboats on the port side of the ship. "Bolin! You have the deck! I trust you have a telepathy stone?"

The helmsman took one hand off the wheel to tap his right ear and give a thumbs-up gesture.

Ahmin took that as silent approval, and climbed into the rear boat as the first one was lowered to the water.

It was only when the admiral's rowboat dropped to the water

that Sunay began to feel the tug of nerves building. Ahmin had always been a stabilizing influence on her, she had discovered, and now she felt truly on her own.

Marco's hand dropped onto her shoulder in an attempt to be comforting. "Now are you ready for a pep talk?"

The joke at least jolted her out of her uncertainty, and she glared daggers at the mage who fell back with a chuckle. She didn't need cheering up. She didn't need encouragement. Ahmin trusted her with an important job, and she was going to *do it*.

Bastard.

"Comin' up on the next drop point!" Bolin shouted. "Juno!"

The spidergirl skipped happily to the port side, then climbed up onto the railing. "Save the boat!" she called out. "I can sneak up easier by swimmin'!"

Juno then dove hands first into the sea, barely leaving even a splash as she entered the water.

Bolin exhaled and muttered to himself, "You'd think I'd have remembered that..." then shouted, "Sunay! Marco! Yer next! Get into position, we'll be swingin' by in ten minutes at most!"

The foxgirl examined her equipment quickly to make sure she had what she needed. A short steel sword hooked to her belt on the left side, and a dagger on her right. A belt pack contained first aid materials: a small spool of wrap, sticky herbs to slow bleeding, and a thumb vial of anti-venom just in case someone on the isle used poisoned darts... or she got bitten by Juno.

She had been trained well not just in combat, but how to *avoid* it if at all possible. She was as ready as she was ever going to be. She looked up over the port side as the *Goldbeard* swung around to the north side of Sacili. She quickly spotted an effective landing point where a raised wooden wall had been constructed as a breakwater. "Right there," she said, pointing it out to Marco "That's where we'll pull up."

The mage nodded, "Good idea. Hopefully our approach won't draw too much attention."

At just that moment, the sound of fighting drifted over the island from the south side. "I'm betting it won't," the foxgirl said. "Let's get in!"

Bolin agreed three seconds later. "Sunay! Yer up!"

"I know that!" She shouted back in annoyance, already halfway into the boat. She sat on the rear bench and situated the oars. She then looked up at Marco, who was nudging her and telling her to move to the front.

"I got the oars," she growled.

Marco replied, "I can do better. Promise."

There wasn't time to argue. If the mage wanted to row, he could be her guest. She moved to the front, sat down, and once Marco had also taken his seat, she gave the thumbs up, and the boat was swiftly lowered to sea level.

"Alright, magic-man, let's see your bulging biceps get to work," Sunay snarked, crossing her arms with a huff.

The mage smiled, and flipped open his book. "Why use muscles when I can use my mind?"

Rowboats normally didn't move in the wind very well; they rested low in the water and didn't have any sails. But when the wind was channeled downward into the stern, that little boat most certainly did move quite quickly, smoothly, and quietly.

"Okay..." the foxgirl reluctantly admitted, "perhaps you do have the right idea."

Marco stilled the wind, allowing the rowboat to drift into their destination behind the breakwater. They hopped out of the boat and were approaching the edge of the wall when they got their first hint that something wasn't right.

*Resistance is harder than anticipated,* Ahmin reported. *Enemy units responding quicker than anticipated and in twice the number. Juno, Sunay, report.*

Juno replied first. *Still swimmin' in, sir. No trouble here yet.*

*Just landed, no sign of trouble either,* Sunay added.

For a man supposedly in the middle of a tougher than expected fight, Admiral Ahmin didn't seem particularly strained. *Then proceed, but with caution. What I've seen so far differs from the intelligence we were given. Be prepared for anything out of the ordinary.*

*Understood,* Juno and Sunay said in unison, then the foxgirl turned to Marco. "The Aramatheans responded to the strike team harder an' faster than we thought. We're gonna have to keep our eyes open."

The mage pointed ahead and upward. "You mean, for up at the top there?"

There were going to be a handful of problems with their ascent, Sunay discovered. The nature of the island gave anybody at the top of the island excellent sight lines... like the twenty Aramathean bowmen circling the base of the Death Ray being guarded by another score of traditional Aramathean Phalanx soldiers with spears and shields.

Before she could report that to the admiral, Juno had bad news of her own. *My target isn't here, admiral! Nor are any designs!*

*There's at least forty men up at the weapon site too,* Sunay added.

Ahmin's voice rarely betrayed emotion, but this time the foxgirl could hear the anger in his voice. *They knew we were coming. They were somehow tipped off. Everyone fall back, and we'll try to regroup. Bolin, we need extraction!*

*Well, we got a little bit of a problem there too,* the helmsman answered. *Three ships are giving us chase, and they've apparently figured out ship-mounted ballistas. We could definitely get all o' ya, but we wouldn't be able to get another shot at this without a* ***lot*** *more manpower.*

Ahmin growled. *Which we won't be able to rouse before this weapon is completed.*

Sunay also figured that a larger scale attack would reveal the Gold Pirates as a legitimate power to be reckoned with, and possibly turn the entire continent on them. They had to do this now... but how?

Juno then interjected again. *I've got four Phalanx moving in towards me. I think I got their attention.*

*Deal with them however you need to,* Ahmin ordered simply. He clearly was out of patience with this unexpected turn of events. *Sunay, Marco, hold your position and we'll push through. If they won't pay us attention, we'll* ***make*** *them pay attention.*

Ahmin was a nigh invulnerable freak of nature, but she doubted even he could overpower the forces on this island by himself, and using the rest of the strike team would no doubt end with a lot of their people dead. There *had* to be a better option, and she had to find it quickly.

"Hey mage," she whispered, "surely you've got somethin' that can take out a lotta guys."

"I'm an illusionist more than an invoker," Marco replied. "I know *some* spells that could do harm, but nothing large enough that could neutralize *all* of them before they turned their weapons on me."

Sunay frowned, and her eyebrows furrowed in frantic concentration. There had to be *something* she could do...

A glimmer of sunlight caught the focusing crystal at the heart of the weapon, and sent a flash of blood red light through the gap created by a Phalanx soldier as he shifted his weight, and that was the inspiration she needed.

"What if I got you a focus crystal?"

Marco snorted. "Then I could probably level half this damn island with a stray thought. But where are you..." then his thoughts ground to a halt as he processed exactly what Sunay was implying. "You're insane."

"You're an illusionist, right?" Sunay explained. "Make me invisible."

"An illusion only works if they aren't expecting it. These people know we're coming."

"If they knew where we were comin' from, don'tcha think they woulda just taken us out by now? I don't think they know exactly how many of us are..."

And then Sunay got a bolt of inspiration. "Better idea. Make me look like, I dunno... how many illusion copies of me do ya think you could make?"

Marco's smile told her all she needed to know.

To the Aramatheans at the top of the island, it must have looked like a hundred foxgirls charging up the hill. Their panicked cries caught the attention of the four soldiers who were closing in on Juno, and in the chaos that followed, Sunay trailed the procession, splitting the ranks that were throwing themselves at air, and nimbly plucked the focus crystal from its golden stand, tucking it under her arm...

Then nearly losing her head to a ball of sizzling fire that zipped right where it would have been had she not seen it just in time to duck. The Aramathean mage was many things, but the two most important right then were that she was an invoker, and could see through the illusion Marco had cast.

Sunay decided to test Marco's claim about spell-casting, and made what would have seemed like a suicidal charge at the mage. But apparently, she wasn't any quicker to cast another spell than Marco would be. The woman in fact panicked, allowing Sunay to slap the book out of her hands and into her face, the foxgirl then using that moment to springboard off the mage's shoulders.

The following jump allowed Sunay to clear the melee, and by the time the Aramathean forces had sorted themselves out, Marco had possession of one sizable focusing crystal.

"Have fun!" Sunay chirped, then contacted Ahmin. *We've got the focusing crystal. Marco's gonna use it to do some damage. Just try and not get killed, okay?*

The admiral replied, *I think we can manage that.*

Marco stepped into the open, but any thought the Aramatheans might have had to attack him disappeared in a hurricane gale force wind that not only sent soldiers spinning, but also bent the mirror array's support beams, knocking them out of alignment or onto the ground where they shattered into irreparable pieces.

The woman mage, while able to hold fast against the wind, was so surprised by the destruction that she turned to assess it and completely forgot about Marco for that split second he needed to cast a second spell, this one a bolt of lightning that crashed directly into the back of her head.

Sunay might have felt sad about witnessing the woman's death if that same woman hadn't tried to flambé the foxgirl's skull a minute earlier.

*Excellent work, Sunay,* Ahmin said, clearly pleased. *Juno, any luck on your end?*

*No sir,* the spidergirl replied in frustration.

Sunay frowned. This wasn't exactly a big island. It's not like he could have gotten too far unless he had a ship...

Her eyes immediately turned to the west, the one area where the Gold Pirates didn't have men stationed, and sure enough, a short, somewhat portly balding man in a toga was moving as fast as he could towards the island's dockside with a scroll case slung over his shoulder.

Sunay smirked, *Juno! West side, the docks! Race ya!*

The spidergirl didn't like those odds. *No fair! Yer closer!*

That much was true, and it was fortunate she was, otherwise Callast might have been able to make it to the boat that was rapidly approaching to retrieve him. Instead, Sunay closed the distance in time to grab him by the back collar of his toga, and yank him off his feet before the Phalanx even could get clear of their boat.

Callast's impact with the ground caused him to lose his grip on the scroll case, which Sunay grabbed herself, deciding that securing the last remaining designs for the weapon were more important than securing a kill. It turned out to be the right decision as well, as Juno arrived on the scene before the engineer could even get back up to his feet, the spidergirl tackling him face first onto the rock and biting him soundly on the neck.

At that point, the Aramathean soldiers were at the end of the docks, charging towards the two chimera, but the fatal damage had been done, and both girls fled at top speed towards the center of the island and the ruined Death Ray. *Callast got bit, Sunay's got the designs.*

*Everyone meet at the south side,* Ahmin ordered. *It'll be a tight fit, but we'll be able to get clear of this hornet's nest faster.*

A tight fit was right as Ahmin jumped into the rowboat next to Sunay as the last man to hop in. The pair had to take one oar each in order to get back to the ship, the poor little boat barely sitting above the water with Jacques and Gurgn making up the rest of the occupants. It only got more difficult considering the *Goldbeard* had to keep moving in order to evade the pursuing Aramathean ships and their mounted ballista.

Gurgn secured one lift rope to the bow end, and Sunay wriggled around Ahmin, perching herself on the edge of the stern in order to secure the rope there. She nearly lost her balance when they were jerked upward, and could hear the straining of the crew trying to pull them aboard.

The crew on the deck must have gotten some help soon after because the straining sounds quieted and the ascent of the rowboat increased. Sunay jumped to the *Goldbeard's* railing the instant she was able, and Juno sighed in relief, "Oh thank the Coders! We should be fine now that we don't have to heft Sunay's weight!"

Sunay sneered mockingly and moved to help on the ropes, but that point the last rowboat was already being secured to the rail, and Ahmin jumped off, landing with a heavy thud on the deck. "Bolin! Full sail! Two hundred and thirty degrees! We'll adjust our course when we're clear! Marco, can you give us a good illusion?"

Marco scoffed. "With this crystal, I could give you a *fleet.*"

Ahmin stared the mage down, then in four strides loomed over Marco. "I would *strongly* suggest that you not get used to possessing that little toy. In fact, why don't you give it to me right this instant?"

The admiral held out his hand expectantly, and Marco quickly realized the wisdom in complying. "Here ya go!" the mage said with a smile, and dropped the blood-red object into Ahmin's hand.

"Very good," Ahmin replied. "Now, prepare for your illusion. Bolin, hard to port to one hundred and eighty degrees once Marco gives the word! Jacques, Sunay... follow me."

Sunay was again surprised that the admiral was summoning her. What could he want from her? She took a deep breath and fell into step behind the first mate, knowing there was only one way to find out.

Ahmin didn't immediately address the pair once he entered the cabin, instead first going to the mysterious metal case, and putting the focusing crystal inside it, a move that confounded Sunay, as it didn't seem like the crystal could possibly fit in terms of width. Nonetheless, Ahmin was able to close and lock the cabinet without trouble, and Sunay knew better than to try and sate her curiosity.

"Sorry about my standoffishness, but I know that mages can get a little... crazy with power. It seemed like the better part of valor to detach Marco from any delusions," he said simply.

The three felt the ship quickly change direction, and braced themselves from falling over. "I take it we're taking him back to Troja?" Jacques asked.

Ahmin nodded in confirmation. "He's got other jobs to do. Even among the Gold Pirates, mages aren't exactly common."

Jacques clicked his tongue in disappointment. "Shame. I could have gotten used to a pocket mage."

Ahmin didn't spare any more small talk, instead turning to Sunay. "When you and Marco approached the weapon site, were you attacked at all?"

Sunay shook her head. "Nope," she said. "They were certainly *waiting* for us, but they didn't advance on our location. They might have known we were comin', but I don't think they knew *where* we were comin' from."

Ahmin sighed in relief. "That was my assessment as well, as they would have had soldiers waiting for Juno as well. That means the leak isn't on this ship, of which I am immensely relieved."

Jacques's voice lost any humor. "But there's definitely a leak somewhere."

"Indeed, and I don't like it. On one hand, while I'm glad I don't have to lose trust in anyone aboard this ship, the network of information for our group is very large, and verifying everyone who might have been able to share our plans with the Aramatheans will take considerable amount of time."

"What do we do in the meantime?"

"All ships in Aramathean waters will operate independently from land operations for now, only contacting our assets ashore when absolutely necessary."

Jacques snorted. "Well, we were used to that during our time in Avalon."

"Only due to incompetence rather than malice," Ahmin corrected. "For now, we will maintain observation of the Void. That's something else we're used to."

"So... no shore leave?"

Ahmin shook his head. "Until we learn more about who is

leaking what information and to whom they are leaking it, this ship, and all others in this section of the fleet, will do nothing but supplying, and only at ports we know are clear."

Sunay's ears flattened, and she couldn't hold back her disappointment.

Jacques didn't seem to like the news at all either, and it was *his* disappointment that caused Ahmin to miss *hers*. "I know, my friend. I know what was promised. But surely you understand."

The first mate nodded, and it was clear he did, even if he didn't like it. It must be a personal matter, as those were ones that were not shared unless offered. As much as Sunay wanted to know, she also knew better than to pry.

"You're both dismissed," Ahmin said. "Thank you for your time."

The pair nodded, but as Sunay turned to leave, the admiral had one more thing to say. "Oh, Sunay. I want to commend you for your efforts on Sacili. Without your quick thinking and quick action, that entire mission would have at best been a tragic success, if not outright failure. I'm sorry that my words are all I can offer in thanks right now."

The praise momentarily buoyed her spirits. Having come to respect Ahmin as a commander *and* as a person in his own right, it felt *very* good to be thanked for her work. "That'll be enough for now, sir," she said, betraying a hint of cheer, then skipped out of the cabin to return to her post.

But the happy rush didn't last long, and the melancholy of uncertainty set in. She only hoped that the parties responsible for this mess were discovered by fall.

# Chapter Ten: Moving On

Sadly, happy news did not come before fall, nor during. Nor even that winter, for what little that particular season meant on the south seas. It wasn't until the following spring that there was any sign that the winds had changed, when Ahmin emerged onto the deck, and took a deep breath with a smile that Sunay could see even with the mask.

"Bolin!" the admiral bellowed with mirth. "Set a course for Grand Aramathea! One hundred and eighty nine degrees, full sail! I want off this boat!"

That got the attention of the entire crew on the deck. Jacques looked especially hopeful. "Does that mean..."

The admiral shrugged. "Message from the Administrator in Grand Aramathea simply said that the matter is being dealt with, and that we are clear to come ashore. I'm not going to quibble the semantics, are you?"

"No, sir."

"Then full sail, Juno! Let's set our feet on some solid land!"

A rousing cheer from the crew both on and below the deck was a clear agreement with that sentiment, and within two minutes, the *Goldbeard's* sails caught the wind and the currents, turning north along with the winds of spring. Sunay's heart jumped into her throat, anticipating with equal parts hope and fear what could possibly be waiting at the capital city of The Imperial Aramathea.

Sailors though they may be, a wooden deck can only sustain a person's feet for so long before they desperately crave solid earth beneath them.

Sunay tried to force those emotions down before they turned into an unstoppable up and down wave. There wasn't even any guarantee that Rola had got word at all, much less had it sent and delivered. She was only offering a *guess* as to when she *might* have found news.

That helped Sunay rein in her emotions about as much as could be expected. Not at all.

Thus began the most painfully long week of Sunay's life to that point from the edges of the living water all the way to the port of destination. Each day, Sunay found herself gazing over the

*Goldbeard's* bow, thinking she could see the diamond glimmer of the cliffs that the First Capital rested upon. She had been fooling herself, and she even knew it, and was always disappointed when she accepted the truth.

Her antics might have earned a bit more grief if Jacques hadn't shown equal anticipation of their coming shore leave. The *Goldbeard's* first mate was a naturally reserved sort, talking about himself very little even to the crew that he had served with for over a decade. She knew his family was initially from northern Avalon, and his immediate family left before the Revolution turned everything upside down... and that was about it.

So seeing him so visibly excited was both a source of humor and of curiosity. Sunay tried to subtly suggest she was willing to listen, but he had not been inclined to approach her. She supposed she could understand that, as she hadn't told anyone about Laron outside of the admiral.

But she eventually forgot about her curiosity once the shimmering face of the diamond cliffs *did* come into view. Morning had just cracked over the horizon, setting the diamond colored shelf into a rainbow of colors. It was probably the most beautiful sight Sunay had ever seen.

Well, the similar effect outside of Tortuga might have compared, but the bitter cold up north dampened the mystique.

"How are we gonna get up there?" Sunay asked. There was a dock that she could barely see, but there wasn't an access to the top of the cliff anywhere.

"There's a boardwalk that slowly climbs the cliff face both for loading and unloading," Jacques explained. "It can be hard to see from a distance, and it can take a while to get to the top, but it's there."

"Why even build such an important city there anyway?"

"It's a remarkably defensible position. Excellent sight of invading forces both from the north *and* from sea. Just burn down the boardwalk and it could take naval invaders a week, if not longer, to get back to the city."

"Hunh." the foxgirl eventually said. "Would be rough if they were ever besieged though."

The first mate shrugged. "There really isn't a *good* place to be under siege."

"True enough."

Jacques then turned his attention towards the business of getting ready to approach the dock. "Juno! Main sails only! Garth, get the starboard gangplank ready and then get to the anchor. Sunay, let Gurgn know to have the row men ready to help slow us down, then let the admiral know we're on our approach."

Juno literally jumped from the main mast to the aft without ever touching the deck, drawing up the sails as she swiftly climbed upward, and Garth had already pulled the gangplank from where it was slotted between the rail and deck on the starboard side by the time Sunay had even reached the stairs below decks. At the bottom, she stuck her head around the entry, and shouted, "All hands to the oars! We're on our approach!"

The foxgirl didn't even wait to see if anyone had responded, the frantic shuffling was enough. She vaulted the steps to the third level two at a time, and sprinted across the hall to the fore side, and swiftly rapping on the door to Ahmin's cabin. "Admiral, we're on our approach."

"Thank you, Sunay," was the muffled response. She could also hear *another* voice that she didn't recognize, but it was far too quiet to make anything out.

"Sir?" she finally asked. "Is everythin' alright?"

"It's fine, Sunay. I have some quick matters to attend to. Go ahead and dismiss the crew."

He was telling *her* to dismiss the crew? "Sh... shouldn't Jacques do that?"

The admiral's voice started to reflect annoyance. "If I wanted Jacques to do it, I would have told you that, don't you think?"

Sunay didn't want to argue, especially since it didn't sound like Ahmin was inclined to do so. "O... okay. See ya up there..."

The foxgirl quickly retreated to the deck, and caught Jacques attention. "The admiral... wants me to dismiss the crew."

The first mate grinned knowingly. "You helped me plan the crew rotation last evening, remember? You know who's on first call don't you?"

Sunay nodded.

"Well then there shouldn't be a problem. Go ahead and call the crew up."

It helped that Jacques didn't have a problem ceding that authority. Even if it *was* merely a ceremonial one, the chain of command was a *very* important thing on a ship. Even the appearance that someone was stepping out of line could cause problems among people in very close quarters.

The foxgirl stopped at the entry of the second deck, and called out, “We are approaching Grand Aramathea. Those on first call, be ready to go to your assigned stations. Everyone else, get topside or get left behind!”

She repeated that call on the third and fourth decks as well, then fell in line behind the people making a similar climb, catching one fellow trying to slip out on his duty in the process: “Torvo, yer in the mess for the first rotation and you know it! Get down there!”

The night deckhand stopped in his tracks, and Sunay pushed herself up against the wall and allowed him to pass her. “Don't worry,” she whispered in sympathy as he passed, “I'm told the night life in Grand Aramathea is more fun anyway.”

Sunay hit the deck and gulped when Ahmin wasn't present, and Jacques was making no visible attempt to step into the admiral's role, going as far as to smile and offer her a gesture to take the role herself. She hesitated, closed her eyes, took a deep breath, then walked to the front of the gathered crew.

She expected quiet mumbling, she expected confusion. She got neither. The crew regarded her position with no qualms or questioning. Buoyed by the respect offered, the foxgirl ordered, “All right, folks. I think you know the drill by now, and that goes for *double* right now. Ya better all damn well be on yer best behavior, because all the punishments are gonna be *double* if ya screw up. I trust there won't be any problems.”

“No, ma'am!” the crew shouted in unison. Sunay kinda liked the sound of that.

“Second shift, do *not* be late gettin' back. Either by volunteer or by order, the first shift can't leave until you return, and it wouldn't be at all fair to them if yer all lollygaggin', unless you wanna be first shift for the next shore leave, got it?”

“Yes, ma'am!”

“Alright then, I won't waste any more of yer time. Dismissed!”

The crowd parted around her, then formed a line off the gangplank, cheering happily in unison. Jacques patted her approvingly on the shoulder after the crowd had filtered off, and descended to the dockside himself. That left Sunay to make sure that all of the first shift crew was in place, then make her leave herself.

And she had just about hit that gangplank when Ahmin's voice startled her.

“Sunay. A word, please.”

The foxgirl turned around, and could see apology in the

admiral eyes as he said, "You're probably not going to like this, but I have urgent matters to attend to. Could you manage the first duty shift for me? I'll return before the shift change, and you can have some extra time."

It was posed as a question, but Sunay knew such things weren't really requests. It really didn't matter that she didn't want to. Besides, if Rola had delivered word, it wasn't going to go anywhere within the next few hours. "Alright. Do yer business, sir."

"Thank you. I appreciate it."

Ahmin took the march down the gangplank, and left Sunay to monitor the deck. Watching the ship was a dreadfully boring affair, especially with the shimmering cliffs and boardwalk so close she could smell the earth... her own senses taunting her.

But it was also an important duty. Even in civilized ports, an empty ship might as well invite thieves and stowaways, both of which meant trouble for ships with limited supplies, even large ships like the *Goldbeard*. She knew it was important, knew *someone* had to do it, and that Ahmin wasn't someone who took liberties for frivolous reasons.

And it also meant that time slowed to a crawl as she eagerly awaited *someone's* return. It didn't even have to be Ahmin. Anyone of the "command" crew could suffice, like Bolin or Jacques or Juno. But she damn well *knew* none of them would be returning even one second before their scheduled time.

A small boat with a single mast and sail, painted white with red trim on the railings floated past the *Goldbeard*, barely visible from Sunay's line of sight. It couldn't have been large enough for more than two people, which she confirmed when the boat moored onto the dock about fifty feet ahead of the *Goldbeard's* bow. Two young Aramatheans, a man and woman climbed out, trimmed their sail, tied down their boat, then began their walk to the boardwalk arm in arm.

Could that have been her and Laron... had circumstances been different? Could it still be them if luck was on her side? If the opportunity even arose, could she part ways with this crew and the purpose they served? Would that be fair to him if she couldn't? Was it even worth knowing at all if there was nothing that she could do? Was the hope more important than the truth?

Sunay didn't particularly like getting philosophical, especially when she was bored. That was something for people with a lot more brains and a lot more free time. She forced herself to look away from the happy couple, and instead up towards the top of the cliff. She certainly wasn't going to see anybody appear at the top of the boardwalk, but she could pretend.

Deciding that standing on the deck was only making her impatience worse, she tried to occupy herself by patrolling the boat and checking on the crew still aboard. When that offered barely any distraction, she slowly trudged up to the deck again... to find Ahmin waiting. She swore she hadn't been gone *that* long for him to appear without her seeing him coming. The two men on the deck seemed likewise astounded, like they had just noticed his presence.

Ahmin said, "Thank you, Sunay, you are free to go."

The foxgirl didn't waste any more time wondering how someone so big could move so swiftly and undetected, because she had more important things on her mind. She sprinted down the gangplank, and dropped to all fours the minute she hit the docks, weaving in and around people as she approached the series of boardwalks that would take her to the top of the cliff.

She slowed once on the incline for two reasons: Firstly, there was an ox driven cart that blocked her progress, and secondly, the cliffs looked even prettier up close, and it stole away her attention. It was almost like diamond colored sand rather than actual diamonds, and no doubt why the Aramatheans settled here rather than mining the entire cliff bare. There wouldn't be much value in diamond dust, really.

She wondered what could have caused such a phenomenon, as diamond was awfully hard stuff. It wasn't easily crushed or pulverized. Whatever had done this, be it natural or godly, it was a powerful force that Sunay decided she didn't want to meet face to face.

Sunay got the opportunity to slip around the cart at the next turn, and it allowed the foxgirl to once again pick up her pace. Even then, it was still a long walk due to the nature of the winding boardwalks that didn't have a more direct option that she could access. There *were* ladders, but they were reserved for Phalanx and emergency use only, and Sunay really didn't feel like chancing it and getting in trouble.

While Gold Pirates were *usually* released after no more than twenty-four hours if they were arrested, that didn't mean Ahmin could allow her to stew for however long he wanted. So Sunay took the long, high road. At least it was a pretty one.

At the top of the cliff, there were several gates into the city. One of them was right in the center, blocked by a barricade and several Phalanx soldiers, which led to the tall spires of the Imperial Palace. It was a remarkable sight, each of the fiver towers taller than anything she had ever seen, and constructed from alabaster material. While Morgana's tower in Tortuga might have been more visually stunning, the sheer scale of Grand Aramathea's palace took the prize.

That wasn't her destination, however, nor did she doubt the soldiers would let her through if it was. That *did* however, raise the question of where she *was* supposed to go. She really didn't want to approach one of the many Phalanx standing vigil at the various gates, firstly because they were very busy as it was handling the influx of people going in and out of the city, and secondly because she really didn't want to risk one of those soldiers having been stationed on Sacili half a year ago.

That would be awkward.

The signs didn't help matters either. As far as she could tell, Grand Aramathea didn't have a dedicated merchant or shopping district. The only directions to the west were "Foreign Quarter" and "Lower Quarter", and "Higher Quarter" to the east, with "Imperial Quarter" point to the north through the barricaded gate.

She exhaled in resignation. There wasn't any way around it.

She pulled her bandana down as low as she could, and kept her head down, trying to avoid eye contact as she approached the nearest Phalanx, a woman with her helmet tucked under her arm, preparing to yield her station to her relief. "Pardon me," Sunay asked, "do you happen to know where the Merchant's Guild here is?"

The soldier pointed at the gate she was vacating. "It's in the Foreign Quarter on the north side of the city. I don't remember exactly where, but there are plenty of Phalanx there that would once you get to the quarter itself. Just take the main road north and northeast, and follow the signs to the Foreign Quarter."

"Thank you," the foxgirl said, relieved that she got an answer without incident, parting as quickly as decency allowed. She presented her travel papers, that had been slightly exaggerated to claim her as an unassociated sailor, to the guard manning the city gate, and was allowed to enter the city itself.

There was a high wall between her and the Imperial Quarter, and the main road veered away from that wall towards the heart of the Lower Quarter. She eschewed the advice of the guard, and continued along that side path that followed the wall around the palace and governmental section of the great city.

For all the splendor she had seen in her short glimpse of the palace, the Lower Quarter wasn't nearly as magnificent. It wasn't exactly squalor, though there were certainly some houses that were in extremely poor repair, but there was no charm to them. They were all pretty much the same design with the same materials, the only differences being a splash of color here and there. For the cultural melting pot of the remaining world, she wasn't seeing much culture so far.

But then again, she guessed “Lower Quarter” didn't exactly refer to elevation. This was the part of town where you built cheaply and didn't splurge on trivial matters unless you had a particularly good year. She knew and understood that sort of mentality.

The road ended abruptly, and Sunay found herself momentarily lost, as she had expected it to eventually join with the main street at some point. She had to double back, wandering residential streets trying to find her way back to the main road. Fortunately, at this time of day, those streets were mostly empty, as the people of the city were at work or school.

Though the foxgirl did had to sidestep quickly to avoid running into an Aramathean girl about her age, stomping past with her head down and grumbling something about not wanting to be a silly shoemaker. Sunay stopped, and called back angrily, “Oi! Kinda rude!” but the girl continued on showing no signs of even *hearing* the foxgirl's shout.

It only helped serve Sunay's sour mood as she wandered though winding roads that veered off in directions that made no sense, dead ended with houses in all directions forcing her to wind back, and taking up an hour of her time simply to find the main road that separated the homes from the shops.

The Lower Quarter was a city in its own right, with its own shops and essential goods, and she suspected the other quarters were the same way. Grand Aramathea was as much four cities as it was one, and perhaps by necessity. You could do your daily business without ever leaving the boundaries of the district you were in. The size and scale astounded Sunay, as she merged into the main road packed with people and carts moving in all directions.

There was barely room to breathe on this road, mostly because it was the only way to leave the quarter if the road signs were any indication. Two main roads, one that went from the docks and round the northwest to the Foreign Quarter, and the other that went east and west between the Imperial Quarter and the outskirts of the city, and walls forming the boundary everywhere else.

Crossing under the arch that separated the Lower Quarter from the Foreign was like stepping into an entirely different world. Color was everywhere and the designs were just as varied. She recognized smatterings of Avalonian architecture, as well as buildings that she had never seen before from lands long since gone, mixed about with the traditional Aramathean buildings she had seen in the empire. *This* was the Grand Aramathea she had been expecting. Buildings with tall steeples and gleaming with bronze, domes, and black shingle... painted red, yellow, brown, blue... she was so lost in the sight that she momentarily forgot she had a purpose for her visit.

Directions to the Merchant's Guild were simple enough. Take the main road to the center circle, and look due south to the biggest building on that side of the center. She apparently wouldn't be able to miss it.

She didn't. It would indeed have been *extremely* difficult to overlook the four story brown brick building angled so that the corner was facing the road, flying the flags of all three major empires above the dark stained oak door. She shouldn't have been surprised by its size, considering it was the heart of organized trade in the largest city in the continent, but it was still a bit much to take in.

Sunay made for the door, and it opened into a beautifully furnished foyer, wood stained to a deep red brown with brass railings, candle holders and a chandelier hanging from the high ceiling that revealed all four floors at the south end with multiple stairways servicing all of them.

A semi-circle desk in front of her had seven clerks in white dress shirts and brown vests, each serving a sizable line of people. Initially worried she'd be spending all day just to find out if Rola had even delivered word yet, she was immensely relieved to find spy a smaller desk bearing a sign labeled “Information and Locations” above it, manned by a single clerk with only two people in line.

That line moved so swiftly that both people had been served before Sunay even got there. The clerk was dressed like all the others, and looked almost Aramathean, if not for the slightly lighter skin and coppery hair marking him as more likely Reahtan. His name, etched on a white tag clipped to his vest, also wasn't Aramathean: 'Gughal'.

“Welcome to the Merchants' Guild of Grand Aramathea. Can I be of service to you, miss?” Gughal asked pleasantly, a demeanor that no doubt came from practice and patience rather than earnest geniality.

The foxgirl said, “I was told to expect a message from one of your members in the Free Provinces. Do I need to wait in that line?”

“Not at all, miss. You want the General Post, which is on the second floor, Southwest Room 3.”

Well, that was a general mercy. "Thank ya kindly."

"Have a pleasant day, my lady."

The walk was remarkably long for being enclosed in one building, and she discovered that the line at the post wasn't much better than the one she had feared queuing up for in the foyer. By the time she finally reached the head of the line, she was in almost as frustrated of a mood as the men and women manning the desk.

The clerk serving her looked tired, and his voice reflected a deep fugue. "Can I help you today?" he said flatly, barely looking up from the list he was looking over and checking off. She was honestly amazed his arms hadn't fallen off handing over that crate that had belonged to the last person in line.

"I might have a message from Rola," the foxgirl said.

"Your name?"

"Sunay."

"Proof of Identification, please."

Sunay showed her travel papers to the clerk, and said with a tired exhale of breath, "One moment, please."

The foxgirl didn't know exactly what a moment was, but the length of time that she spent waiting had to have been several. But her heart jumped when the clerk returned with a yellow envelope bearing Sunay's name.

"There is a prompt reply order attached to this message," he said as he handed the envelope across the counter. "So unless you want to get back in line and wait, I would suggest reading it here and composing your response here at the desk."

Sunay had already ripped the envelope open at the narrow edge by the time he had finished speaking.

*Dearest Little Fox,*

*I have news that is both good and bad. My sources in Avalon tell me that your boyfriend's family was not executed or put to the labor camps. Sadly, they were forbidden to return to their home, and were exiled from Avalon instead. Your dear Laron lives. I learned that some of the Gold Pirates themselves helped the family get out of the Republic before it decided to change its mind on its selected punishment, as it is wont to do. That is the good news.*

*They now live, albeit modestly, in the Northern Free Provinces, in a place called Vakulm, to the east of the Great Snake River. and nary a few days from the Daynelands. I will not lie, it is a precarious place, and raids even in the best of times are not uncommon... and I fear that these are not the best of times, and will only get worse. That is the bad news.*

*But what may hurt you deeply, and I shudder to mention it, but I fear I must. Laron has come to fancy one of the agents that helped him escape, and they have grown quite close. Should I mention you to him, let him know that you are well at the very least? Do advise, little fox, for I do not want to cause undue drama. Write a reply and hand it to the clerk. They will know how to get it to me.*

*Sincerely,*

*The Big Bad Wolf*

Sunay felt like she had been punched. For a moment, a flare of betrayal lit in her eyes before sense grabbed her by the throat. There was no reason for Laron to think she was even still *alive.* Besides, it's not like they had been friends for years and tragically parted. He had known her for a handful of months at best. How was it *his* fault that she had conjured flights of fancy that didn't reflect reality?

"Do you have any paper for a reply?" Sunay asked the clerk.

"Yes. And Madam Rola already covered the return cost, so there is no charge to you."

He offered said paper along with a pen. She hadn't seen anything quite like this... a clear pen with in the ink *inside* the barrel. It was so fascinating that she initially forgot she was going to be writing with it. Once she did, she found herself glad for Matron Miriam's teaching, for while she doubted her penmanship was at all that beautiful, she didn't have to shame herself asking the clerk or someone else to write *for* her.

*Dearest Big Bad Wolf,*

*Do not tell him anything about me. If for some reason he asks one of your contacts about me, tell him that I was killed by Avalon Republican Police while trying to flee the country. He's at peace and happy now, he should stay that way.*

*With Thanks,*

*The Little Fox*

Sunay had to wipe her eyes with her sleeve as she handed the reply to the clerk for delivery, but the only thing she regretted about it was that she referred to Rola as "dearest." It was probably a bad idea to encourage the wolf spirit in such a fashion.

The foxgirl thought she might have thanked the clerk in parting, but wasn't certain. She knew she had to get out of that place before she completely broke down, and her eyesight was already starting to blur with tears. Sunay wasn't certain where exactly she was going, and didn't really care. She just wanted to find someplace fairly secluded without a lot of people and have a good cry.

She found that place on the third floor, at the south corner, in front of a meeting hall that was unoccupied. She dropped onto her bottom, curled her knees up against her chest, buried her head in her knees, and started whimpering, shaking herself with her sobs. All the logic in the world wasn't going to help right now. This *hurt*.

She removed the earring, that had been Laron's present and promise to her, and held it in her cupped hands. It had taken a bit of a beating from the salty sea air, but remained intact despite all her adventures. Had it meant nothing to him? Was it just a worthless trinket that he had already forgotten about?

"Bad news, I take it?"

Sunay recoiled, the words reaching her ear coming from so close that her initial instinct kicked in before she could recognize the voice and stop herself from striking Ahmin square in the nose. "Coders! Don't *do* that!" she snarled, then hiccuped as she tried to regain control of her lungs.

"I apologize if this seems incredibly callous, but I do need your help on matters that are exceptionally time sensitive," he said, cutting straight to business. "Can we talk on the way back to the ship?"

The foxgirl forced aside her bubbling, and nodded, accepting Ahmin's hand to help her to her feet. If there was business to be done, and it had to be important if Ahmin was interrupting her leave for it, then Sunay needed to get her wits together quick.

Ahmin led her to a rear exit of the guild hall on the southeast side. "So... what *was* that all about, if I may ask?" he asked as he pushed open the door and held it open for Sunay to step through.

"I got information... about Laron," she said.

"Oh no..."

Sunay shook her head. "It's not like that... it's actually pretty silly that I'm getting so worked up about it. He and his family are alive and reasonably well. He's just... he's moved on."

Ahmin closed his eyes. "That's not much consolation to you, is it? Why shouldn't you be saddened?"

"That's not selfish?"

"It's only selfish if you wish him to feel as badly as you do."

She knew that was supposed to make her feel better. It didn't, but she appreciated the attempt. "Alright, enough about my whimpering. What is the important business?"

"We'll save that for when we're on the ship. There are too many loose eyes and ears in this city for me to be comfortable discussing sensitive matters."

Sunay understood that, and so kept up the small talk even though she didn't want to. "Laron and I got real close real quick. Maybe too quick, I guess," she said, dangling the earring in her right hand. "He gave me this... just before we were gonna run off together. I barely knew him three months, and was ready to run to a foreign land. Stupid, huh?"

"Desperate times lead to desperate measures, and for chimeras in Avalon, these are rather desperate times. Perhaps it was reckless and ill-advised, but it worked out for the best, right? Sometimes... that's the comfort you have to take when there isn't really a *right* decision."

"I guess..." she said. "And if I tell myself that enough, I might just believe it."

"That's the spirit!" Ahmin said.

They shared a short laugh, and Sunay allowed herself to be entranced by the sight as she went down the boardwalk back to the docks. It really was beautiful, seeing the early evening sun reflecting off the water and the cliffs behind them and casting a rainbow of colors across the treated wooden planks of the boardwalk.

She wouldn't trade her time with the Gold Pirates for anything. A quiet life in the Free Provinces or Aramathea wasn't for her. Not yet. Maybe not ever. Maybe Ahmin *was* right, and that it all worked out as well as it possibly could have.

"That earring looks good on you," Ahmin said casually.

Sunay had been torn with just throwing it aside, but hadn't been able to work up the nerve, and the admiral must have noticed that. "Ya think so?"

"Shame to just throw it away. Even if the promise has faded, the memories haven't."

Deciding to accept Ahmin's advice, the foxgirl clipped the jewelry back on her ear. "Very well. I trust yer judgment."

Ahmin picked up his pace as they hit the dock, forcing Sunay to have to occasionally jog to keep up as he made a beeline through the crowd towards the *Goldbeard*. Juno greeted them with a wave and a smile as they went up the gangplank. "Yer not supposed to be back! Does that mean I get a break?"

"Afraid not, Juno. I need to discuss some business with Sunay then we're heading right back out. Don't worry, Jacques will be back by dusk so you can enjoy the nightlife."

"Yay!" the spidergirl chirped.

Ahmin chuckled as he ducked into stairwell. "You would not think she could be the most cold-blooded killer on this entire boat."

Sunay agreed. "I sometimes forget that, and I've slept below her for almost a year."

The humor dried up the moment Ahmin closed the door to his cabin. He sat down onto his bed, hands folded in front of his face. "This is the deal, Sunay. Our leak in the organization is at work in Grand Aramathea."

"I thought that was settled," Sunay replied.

"Yes, that's what I thought too. Then I learned it's because the Administrator in Grand Aramathea took assumptions that I am rather displeased with, but feel inclined to pass on."

Now Sunay wondered what that had to do with her. Before she could ask, Ahmin answered for her.

"You made a bit of a name for yourself on Sacili, both among the Gold Pirates *and* with whoever our leak is. Your description is floating around Grand Aramathea, though the Phalanx so far haven't been showing much interest, and there are a number of potential suspects as to who could have done it. The Administrator for The Imperial Aramathea wants *you* to serve as bait to lure our leak out... hence his assumption, considering he didn't clear any of this with me, and least of all *you.*"

Ahmin was *not* happy about this, and it showed as he dropped his hands and clenched his fists. "Courtesy tells me to pass that along, but I also wish to impress upon you that you are *not* his asset. You are under *my* authority, and if you do not wish to do this, I will be more than happy to tell my colleague in just what orifice he can insert the nearest candlestick."

Sunay took a deep breath, because she really *didn't* like people speaking for her, but... "The alternative is to go back out into sea with minimal contact with the shore, isn't it?"

Ahmin cringed as he admitted, "Yes."

"Then I'll do it. I ain't gonna like it, but I'll do it."

The large pirate sighed in relief. "I appreciate your assistance, although I'll admit I would have been content telling the Administrator very specific ways he could fornicate with himself."

Sunay shrugged. "Just remind him on occasion that he needed the Fleet to plug his own leak."

Ahmin's eyes lit up. "Oh, that's brilliant. At any rate, here..."

The foxgirl's ears flattened when Ahmin reached into the metal cabinet, and handed her a telepathy stone. "Ugh, I *hate* these..."

"I know, but we need to be able to remain in contact with you. We'll be backtracking through the connections, because we're reasonably certain there is a chain of informants going on here, and so you are likely going to have to keep whoever approaches you busy while we do that. The longer our leak's eyes are on you, the better.

"We've let word slip that you'll be spending at least part of the night at The Grue, a tavern in the Northwest of the Foreign Quarter. Our plan is to see who approaches you, and if they are connected to one of the suspects our agents on shore have compiled. They believe once they are able to make that connection, that the network will unravel from there."

Sunay grunted in response. "Unless that someone turns out to be a whole unit of Phalanx that levels the entire bar."

"That is *highly* unlikely," Ahmin replied. "As I mentioned, the Phalanx in the city haven't shown much interest in the information, which suggests the leak is someone outside that chain of command. But the leaks have been showing specific interest in you, however, and might be willing to approach you if you make yourself accessible. No,

I'm not sure why they believe that."

He paused for a moment in thought, then added, "Though it *is* possible whoever it is has earned some points with the Phalanx by correctly predicting the attack on Sacili..."

She was already regretting agreeing to this plan.

~ ~ ~ ~ ~

Her mood didn't improve as the scheme churned into action either.

It wasn't the tavern's fault. It was actually a pretty nice establishment, if plain. She had certainly experienced worse places.

The beer wasn't particularly great, but she had come to expect that. In addition to her improving alcohol tolerance, Aramathean brews were notoriously weak. It was a shame because she would have *liked* to have a good buzz going by now, but that wasn't so much the problem, either.

Sunay discovered she *really* didn't like the landlubber operations of the Gold Pirates. Their secretive nature lent itself to scenarios such as these, it would seem... where *someone*, at *some time*, was going to do *something* about her. It was possible that this someone (or some*ones*) wasn't even going to make their move *here*.

Coders, she didn't even know who *her* people were in all this.

She was used to the *Goldbeard*, where she knew everyone by name. Right now, she felt completely alone, even if Ahmin's voice occasionally rung in her ear. She didn't like this feeling at all.

*It might not hurt if you looked more approachable. Right now you look like you're about to bite the first person who enters your range.*

At least the admiral was close enough to be watching, though she couldn't figure out how. Ahmin rather stood out.

*Well, that's good, because that's exactly how I feel*, she replied.

*Then try not to. You won't get the chance to bite anyone if you don't let them get close enough.*

Sunay growled silently, but nonetheless perked up her ears and straightened her back. While she doubted anyone who had ill intent for her would be dissuaded by her posture, she supposed it didn't hurt to play the game how her shadowy leaders wanted it.

The bartender dropped another glass in front of her, and she fought back the urge to regard it distastefully. It took her a moment to get over the sight of the distressingly weak pale amber liquid before she realized she didn't order this.

"Oi!" the foxgirl hissed, pointing down at the small glass. "This ain't mine."

"The man in the corner table over there bought it for you," the bartender answered, pointing to the southwest, where a solitary man commanded a small booth by the glass window that looked out to the main road. He stood directly under a series of candles, which cast him in surprisingly clear lighting considering the time of day, allowing Sunay a very good look at him.

He was a remarkably unassuming fellow, brown canvas trousers, with a similarly colored long sleeve shirt and vest. His features were of a typical Aramathean male, soft, olive-skinned, brown eyes and dark brown hair, with nothing particularly unique, no scars, tattoos, or anything else.

Everything about him said "perfectly average," which perhaps ironically was what made him so very suspicious.

She was already sliding out of her stool as Ahmin ordered, *Go to him.* She took the drink he purchased, and with slow deliberate steps crossed the lobby floor, weaving through people and tables, finally locking eyes with her quarry as she was within feet of the booth.

The foxgirl sat at the empty seat across from him. From this distance, she could smell his nervousness despite his face remaining calm. "I do apologize if I startled you, miss, but I rarely see such exotic beauties around here," he said candidly. It was very easy to sound creepy while trying to be friendly to strangers; that he didn't immediately set off alarms in Sunay's head told her it was either genuine or carefully practiced.

And this situation didn't particularly lend itself towards genuine.

"Grand Aramathea is the meeting point of all the world's cultures," Sunay replied coyly. "I think you speak false."

"Foxes are rare in the empire," he answered. "Ever rarer to see them blessed upon a lady."

Sunay's eyes narrowed playfully. "I think I'm going to need your name before I go too much further into this game."

The man sounded genuinely contrite, even to her ears. "Oh goodness, here I am trying to be charming, and I forget the most common part of decency. I'm Cassus, a mere scribe, which is probably why I don't think much of my name and profession."

*Got it,* Ahmin's voice said. *Checks out, scribe for the Imperial Library, journalist for the Aramathean Journal... and* ***not*** *one of the* *names on our lists of suspects.*

Sunay maintained her smile and eye contact even as she mentally asked, *Want me to bail out?*

*No. It just means we need to expand our list. Might take time, so keep him busy.*

Sunay broadened her smile and internally screamed. How she longed for the fleet business that went precisely as it was supposed to.

*I have ears, woman,* Ahmin snarled.

Now the smile was genuine. It hadn't been her intent for that mental howl to be something Ahmin heard, but that he did was a nice bonus. She turned her focus back to Cassus. "Sunay. It's a pleasure."

"I know, in fact," he said, an admission that even startled Ahmin, judging from the curious hum in Sunay's ear. It was definitely an odd turn in this supposed game to reveal something of that nature so quickly. "Your name and description have been floating around the Aramathean Journal. I was curious to see what the interest was about. Now I do."

She leaned forward, dropping her elbows on the table, and resting her chin on her hands. Sunay wasn't normally one to call attention to her... assets... but knew how to do so if needed, and certainly fully intended for the neckline of her shift to drop and reveal a hint of cleavage. "Oh, and what do they say about me?"

*Good, keep him talking,* Ahmin said. *We might just have an angle here even if he isn't one of our suspects.*

"Nothing specific. Just whispers among my colleagues of a foxgirl named Sunay arriving in Grand Aramathea for ears not meant to be mine. I was curious about what all the talk was about. Now I know."

Sunay suspected Cassus's fellows were chatting about the events on Sacili rather than her stunning visage. Chimeras rarely got that sort of attention, even if they were strikingly beautiful. And while Sunay didn't think she was at all ugly, she also knew bards weren't going to be composing sonatas about her freckled face, either.

"You might not hear this much, but *I* find chimeras enchanting."

"Yer right, I don't." Only... only... from someone who has since moved on.

"Then it is a loss for the rest of the world," Cassus said, reaching over to touch her arm. "Though in the spirit of fairness, I *am* a scribe by trade, and I am just as fascinated to learn what makes you so interesting to my colleagues, because I do not think they share my tastes."

*Play along for now,* Ahmin advised. *We're trying to match members of the Journal with any of our suspects. Just string this as long as you can. The longer they think we're prying into this clown, the longer they'll think we're completely off track. We might be able to catch them with their guard down.*

"Well, all I can say is that I can't imagine why they would know me or why they would find me so interesting. I'm just a mercenary sailor, sailing with a shipping crew from the Free Provinces. There was some drama about my heritage in Avalon, but I doubt that would be what caught their ear."

"It's caught mine... among other things."

Sunay had to fight from rolling her eyes, even though he wasn't lying. Humans, just like every other animal, had a musk, a scent that distinctly betrayed arousal. It wasn't quite as *strong* as a wolf or a fox, to be sure, but it was there, and even a normal human's nose could pick up on it, though unconsciously.

"Well, if ya *must* hear about my misadventures in my homeland, I suppose I can entertain ya." It was an innocuous enough of a topic, really, certainly nothing that would jeopardize Gold Pirate activities, and would no doubt keep this fellow's ear.

"Perhaps we can entertain each other somewhere a little more... private? And... higher class?" Cassus offered. "No offense to the clientele at this establishment, but it really isn't suitable for more than a cheap drink."

*Just how far am I supposed to "entertain" this boy?* Sunay queried.

*Entirely up to you. Apparently there are agents running about checking every connection under the sun. If it gets too much for you and they aren't done, that's their problem as far as I'm concerned.*

She knew she was probably going to regret this. She knew she was probably only going further with this scheme because she wanted to "get back" at Laron for "betraying" her. But why not? She wasn't a matron. She had no intention of being one either, and Cassus was hardly ugly. *Tell them they'll have* ***all*** *the time they need.*

"Why, that sounds like a great idea, Mister Cassus," Sunay finally said with a smile and a purr. He stood, offered her his arm, and when she took it, led her out into the night streets of Grand Aramathea.

He stuck to the well lit roads, no doubt out of habit, though with her it probably wouldn't have mattered. He also wasn't kidding about "someplace higher class" either, as he made a path towards the arch that separated the Foreign from the Higher Quarter.

There wasn't a single building under two stories in the Higher Quarter as far as she could tell. And she also doubted more than one family lived in any of them. They were also of quality manufacture, with brilliant white stone and fire-hardened clay shingles on their roofs. The streets were impeccable, smooth gray cobblestone with nary even a lose pebble or piece of litter.

"It's amazing that for a city that prides itself on a melding of cultures that it can be so damn uniform," Sunay noted.

"That's the Higher Quarter for you. As a rule, my fellows look on the foreign elements with disdain, even as we reap the benefits of the trade it brings," Cassus replied.

"You're one of *these* people, eh?"

Cassus shook his head, "In name, I suppose. My brother embraces the Higher Citizen life more than I do. Though I suppose I can't hate it too much, all things considered."

Said home looked like all the others on the surface, three floors of immaculate craftsmanship with an astonishingly spacious lawn of neatly trimmed grass considering they were in the middle of the largest city left in the world. It wasn't the largest home in the quarter, or even on the block, but it likely had more value than every room she had ever slept in combined.

"It's not much comparatively, but a lot more than most everyone else has. Come on in."

Cassus pushed open the maple wood door, polished with a glossy finish that glimmered in the dim candlelight from the road. Inside was marble floors, brown wool throw rugs, obviously expensive oil paintings in gold leaf frames, and in the living room three white leather lounging couches with plush cotton pillows of the same color that flanked a covered fire pit.

He escorted Sunay to one of the couches, and held up one finger to ask her to wait. "I'll be right back."

The foxgirl snuggled into the cushions and pillows, figuring she might as well live it up while she can. She probably wasn't going to feel comfort like this ever again. Cassus returned with a dark tinted bottle filled with what she guessed was a red liquid. "A Reahtan Red, my family would probably disown me for the sacrilege, but the look on your face when presented with our drinks suggested you wanted something with a bit more bite."

"Observant *and* civilized? I am likin' this," Sunay said in approval as he set a narrow necked glass down at the glass table in front of her and poured her a liberal portion of the wine in question. It was a tart grape almost entirely covered up by an alcoholic sting. "Mmm... distilled, I see. The Reahtans know how to make a good wine."

"And the Avalonians good women," Cassus said as he took a seat across from her.

Sunay snorted, "Not much of a charmer, but at least yer tryin'." She then gave her surroundings an exaggerated look around, and said, "Wonderful place. I feel awfully underdressed for such a fine establishment in these tattered ol' rags o' mine."

Cassus would have to be blind, deaf, and dumb to not get the hint. Fortunately, he was neither, though he played along. "I could see if I have something that would fit you, though between my brother and I, we don't exactly have clothes that would be proper for a lady," he said, then paused before adding, "At least, not since that time our grandmother walked in on my brother playing dress-up. That was an awkward time."

Sunay grinned predatorily as she stood, crossing the distance as she pulled her shirt over her head and dropped it to the floor, hands working behind her to untie the wrap over her chest. "Well, I hope this won't be awkward. I'd hate to have to wasted your time while I still have so many stories to tell."

"There will be plenty of time for tales of foreign lands later," Cassus declared, standing to meet Sunay as she rounded the table, wrapping his arms around her back as the wrap fell off her body.

And then the door was nearly kicked straight off its hinges, and five Phalanx burst through, led by a man that Cassus clearly knew, if the family resemblance hadn't been enough to tip her off.

Cassus pushed Sunay away and she scrambled for her shirt as the pair was surrounded. "Damn it, Daneid, we were over this. I get her to tell me the code, *then* you burst in to arrest her."

"What? What code, you..." Sunay began, before a spear head pointed between her eyes, courtesy of Daneid.

"Plans change, brother. Your pithy conspiracy theories can wait."

The soldier's eyes widened when he finally got a good look at Sunay, fixating on her bandana. "Void take it..." he then glared at his brother, and gestured to Sunay with his spear. "Get her shirt on and take her away," he ordered his men. "We have no more than twenty-four hours with this woman, and I don't want to waste a second of it."

## Chapter Eleven: Moving Up

Gold Pirates had three rules for when they were apprehended by law enforcement.

1) Shut up, and don't say or do anything.

2) You won't be there long.

3) If there are any questions, refer to Rule #1.

It also meant that she had the most boring night in the history of the world. Every two hours, Lieutenant Daneid would approach her cell, demand answers to his questions, then stomp away furious when she refused to answer them. By the third time, she started messing with him, and she had every intention of continuing to do so when he showed up a fourth time.

"Listen, boy, if yer jealous, I'd be more than willing to give ya what I was about to give yer brother," she said, leaning back against the rough brick of her cell in the First Phalanx prison in the Lower Quarter, because of course, the Higher Quarter wouldn't be saddled with something like a jail. That would harm property values. "You don't have to keep visitin' me and playin' coy."

Daneid was a true Phalanx officer, he refused to be shoved off course no matter what Sunay said or did. "I demand to know what your next target is."

Gold Pirate crews didn't even know their next *port* for precisely this reason. But even if she did know, she certainly wasn't going to tell this golden boy. This was a dance they had done enough times, she'd think he'd be tired of it by now, "Again, I don't know what yer talkin' about."

"Like the pits you don't," Daneid snarled. "I had friends on Sacili. And I know you were there."

"You don't know nuthin'."

"Some of those friends are dead."

"Damn shame." If he was expecting Sunay to be sad about some mooks getting killed, he had another thing coming.

"I have friends from since we were children stationed all over the empire," Daneid continued, "and I will do anything I can to help preserve their lives if I can." Turning to the guard at the cell, he ordered, "Open it."

*This* was a deviation from the normal routine. Daneid stepped inside, and Sunay stepped up to meet him. Physically, it was a bit of a mismatch, he had her by a good five inches in both height and width.

"I have little patience for your games. You *will* tell me what your crew's next target is."

Sunay snarled, "And I'm tellin' ya I don't..."

At that point, Daneid's face contorted in rage, and he shoved Sunay against the wall, causing the back of her head to bounce painfully off the brick. While stars swam through her eyes, Daneid pulled her off the ground and threw her back onto the cot in her cell. "I don't want to hear any more of your lies!"

He lorded over the foxgirl, who curled up defensively even as she remained defiant. "Helena, Baccari, Valus... you don't know those names, I do. All three will never be coming home because of you and your pirates."

"And smackin' me around ain't gonna send them home, either," she spat angrily and her reward for that remark was getting picked up and thrown across the cell like a rag doll.

She anticipated something of the sort however, going limp this time and tucking her head forward. So when Daneid approached this time, she was anything but dazed, pouncing forward and taking him off guard. As a result, Daneid was caught mid-stride, losing his balance and his neck caught the edge of the cot.

The Phalanx officer howled in pain, and crumpled, but before Sunay could take any advantage, she was thrown off Daneid and tackled to the stone floor with a blade pressing against the back of her neck. Daneid shoved them away and grabbed Sunay under her shoulders, picked her up, and pinned her against the wall with her hands behind her back.

With guards as backup, Sunay wasn't going to be able to put up much of a fight. She really shouldn't have tried to begin with, and Ahmin would no doubt give her an earful for it, but listening to that cad's howl was worth it.

"I have some powerful friends myself, pirate," Daneid hissed. "Maybe I'm willing to take my chances that my influence is a bit stronger than yours."

"You would think wrong, Lieutenant."

The female voice that came from the open cell door was

extremely certain of that fact. Sunay couldn't see who that person was until Daneid peeled away to address the woman in question. "General Helena?"

A female general? Sunay thought as she turned about. She wasn't the typical Aramathean, with copper shoulder length hair and blue eyes despite bronzed skin. She wasn't particularly all that feminine either, with well toned muscles visible underneath the leather skirt.

"I'm here to take custody over your prisoner and release her to her proper authority. I figured you'd resist a messenger," Helena declared, her voice barely above a growl.

"But... General..."

Helena's eyes narrowed. "Lieutenant, I understand, which is why I'm not demanding you lay down your spear right this instant. But our orders are clear on this matter. The pirate comes with me. Miss Sunay? To me. Move quickly."

The foxgirl sneered with a healthy display of teeth as she passed the Lieutenant and to the general's side. Helena was even bigger up close, a towering specimen that Sunay would have believed was a man if not for the face and slight curve in the general's breastplate.

Helena spun full about on her right heel, and said simply, "Follow. Now."

Sunay fell in step, and tried to say, "Thank ya for..."

"I want to release you less than the Lieutenant does," Helena snapped, turning her head to eye Sunay coldly, "but I'd rather not be demoted by defying the Venerated Judge's order."

Sunay gulped as Helena's biceps visibly flexed. "U... understood."

They passed by the foreman's office, which surprised Sunay as she had started to turn towards it to finalize the paperwork for her release. After scrambling to catch up the general's long strides, she was told, "You were never officially here, by order of the judge. As a result, there's nothing for you to sign. That's how it works with your kind, though I have no idea why. How did you not know that?"

The foxgirl shrugged indifferently, but otherwise said nothing. She doubted Helena would believe the truth that Sunay had never been arrested before anyway.

The sun was up by the time she emerged outside the jail, blinking her eyes repeatedly to try and adjust to the drastic shift in lighting. Once successful, she couldn't decide to be happy or annoyed that only Ahmin was waiting for her. On one hand, she was relieved to see what she knew was a friendly face. On the other, it annoyed her that she still had no idea exactly who she had been working with the entire operation.

"Have fun?" Ahmin asked, his voice teasing. "Ya know, we tell our agents *not* to cause trouble while in custody for a reason."

Sunay huffed unrepentantly. If Ahmin was legitimately upset about her scuffle, he wouldn't bring it up right now in public. "He deserved it."

His only response was a quiet laugh.

"This had better have been worth our trouble," Sunay added with a growl as she followed his silent gesture to his side.

"Not as worth it as I would have hoped," the admiral replied, taking the road back towards the docks. "But better than our colleagues expected, I am led to believe."

Sunay figured she might as well know the details. "How's that?"

"Your friend Cassus wasn't tied to our leak, as we suspected. But he's also not much of a journalist either, which is why the people who *were* leaking Gold Pirate information didn't think much of him lingering about and overhearing their information trade."

"But we found the agent responsible?"

Ahmin nodded, "Eventually, yes... which is why it regrettably took so long to get to you. It was actually one of the Administrator's top assistants, and we wanted to make sure we had this person dead to rights before we snapped the trap shut. I am sorry."

"Not yer fault," Sunay replied. "Just glad we got the bastard so that I can get some sleep."

Ahmin laughed, and the foxgirl allowed herself a tired smile. "Yeah, let's get you back to the *Goldbeard*."

But Sunay had one last question once they were on the safety of the ship. "Cassus mentioned something about a code. What was he prattling about?" she asked, giving Bolin a nod in greeting once they were on the deck.

Ahmin went awkwardly silent, his eyes regarding Sunay warily, as if he wasn't exactly sure how or even *if* he could answer that question. At the end of that long pause, he finally said, "He was no doubt referring to the authentication Administrators and their assistants use in order to communicate amongst ourselves, though why he thought you would know it is beyond my guess. *Why* he thought it could be of use to him is a bit more troubling... and makes me think I need to make another contact with our agents on the ground."

Sunay knew she was overstepping her bounds, but... "Can I ask why?"

Another long pause, and gestured for Bolin to give them some space. When the helmsman complied, the admiral lowered his voice. "It's probably nothing, but it's a little too close together for it to be mere coincidence. The administrators and their assistants have specific relics that they use, relics that are unique to those people and are *supposed* to be destroyed when they resign."

Sunay knew what "supposed" implied.

Ahmin confirmed it. "However, we are discovering these supposedly destroyed artifacts popping up. Fortunately, no one who has been finding them has figured out what to do with them. I know one of them popped up at a black market auction nearly a month ago, but that it was sold before our agents could secure it."

"You're worried Cassus knew who bought it, and knew the code could be used to access it."

"It would be the most devastating access not only to Gold Pirate operations, but potentially to secrets of the world not meant for mortal eyes."

Sunay groaned. "So where are we goin' now?"

Ahmin shook his head. "It's not our problem. That's for our agents on land to handle."

"Well, I'm inspired with confidence now."

"Their job can be a lot harder than ours, Sunay," the admiral chided before he added, "But I won't disagree with you on this one."

Sunay yawned again, and she decided that was as good of an indicator to stop talking and find her way to her cot. "Alright, I'm gonna go pass out now. That all right with you, sir?"

"Get some shut eye, Sunay. I need you awake for tonight."

That caused the foxgirl to cock a tired eyebrow. "What for?"

Her commanding officer's eyes glimmered playfully. "It's a surprise."

Sunay's eyes narrowed. "And this is supposed to help me sleep *how*?"

Ahmin shrugged in response.

Knowing she wasn't going to get anything more out of the admiral, Sunay grumbled as she made her way below deck and to her cot. The foxgirl hated surprises for the most part, and that anxiety would have under normal circumstances kept her awake dreading what was coming. But being awake for over twenty-four hours and all the adrenaline burned during the events of said day overcame anything else, and she collapsed face down onto her cot, asleep nary an instant after her head dropped onto her pillow.

~ ~ ~ ~ ~

It was a dreamless sleep, or at least no dream she could remember. This was a good thing, as far as she was concerned, having expected some gloomy nightmare featuring Laron.

"Hey, wake up! Come on now! Ya don't wanna be late!"

Juno was a morning person. *And* a night person, as far as Sunay could tell.

"Ahhmmmup..." Sunay grumbled, swatting in the general direction of the spidergirl's voice as she pushed herself up to her elbows, rolled over, and used her left hand to wipe crust out of her eyes. "What time is it?"

"Five hours past by local reckonin'," Juno replied. "We wanna get to the Silver Doubloon within an hour."

"Where's that?" Sunay really didn't want to know, she really wanted nothing more than another hour of sleep. "Wake me up in a half hour."

"It's in the Lower Quarter, but I'm afraid I can't let ya. Everyone has to come. Mandatory meetin' and all."

"Then who's gonna watch the ship?"

"The admiral has it covered. Got the support of the local Phalanx. Guess they're *real* apologetic about somethin'."

Sunay slid out of her cot, and straightened her clothes. "Probably wants me in my best, eh?"

The "best" clothes really didn't mean much on the *Goldbeard*. It was the set of clothes the least beat up by the workday. It meant canvas trousers that didn't have holes in the knees and a gray shirt that only had two stains on the collar and no missing buttons.

"That reminds me that we need to pick up some buttons for ya, huh?" Juno quipped as the foxgirl put on said shirt. "You keep poppin' them off, aren'tcha?"

Sunay glared at the spidergirl. "My chest ain't *that* big."

Juno grinned as Sunay then promptly sucked in a breath so that she could fit the top two buttons into their respective slits, earning her another warning glare.

"Not. A. Word."

Juno made a zipping motion across her mouth, even as the

cheeky grin remained.

Sunay stepped into her "best" shoes, glad for the excuse to wear something without a completely worn sole, and grumpily walked past Juno before stopping. "Yer the one who knows where we're goin', right?"

"Yep!" the spidergirl replied. "I was wondering why you were takin' the lead!"

Sunay took one step to her left. "Then hurry up so we can get this over with and I can go back to sleep."

The walk roused the foxgirl though, helped by the slight tint of surprisingly cool air coming from the north once they had scaled the boardwalk and onto the cliff top. The sun was starting its shift to amber and giving the surroundings a stunning orange glow on the mostly pale stucco buildings.

If she didn't know better, she would have thought such a sight was why denizens of the Lower Quarter didn't paint their homes.

"It *is* pretty, isn't it?" Juno asked, though with a tone that didn't expect an answer. "Almost reminds me of *my* home, though without the crazy cultists and bloody sacrificial rituals."

Juno rarely talked about her early years outside of what she had to, so Sunay seized the opportunity. "How so?"

"The cave that I was hidden in faced out to the Eastern Forever Sea. Every morning, the sun would cast this same golden glow into the cave's interior. I was afraid of it at first, until... until the Admiral and his crew pulled me out of there."

"Did he ever tell you why?"

Juno shook her head, "Nope. Just that I was Chosen, and had been from a very young age. I wasn't gonna be any herald of murder, I was gonna be myself."

"With his crew."

Juno turned to face Sunay, the spidergirl squinting in the light. "I couldn't explain it, but it felt right, ya know?"

Sunay understood that. "Yeah, I suppose it did."

"Just like it felt right for ya when ya took charge, right?"

The foxgirl cringed. She had been a fool to think that little event had gone without any pushback. Of *course* she'd have issues with that authority usurped by the new girl.

Juno sensed that reaction, and immediately sighed. "Oh, come off it. If I had a problem with ya takin' *that* little ceremony, I'd have said so then and there, and ya know it. It was an honest question. Don't need to be shy."

That didn't really help Sunay's nerves any, but she answered as honestly as she could. "Well... no one seemed to have a problem with it, did they?"

"Nope," Juno confirmed.

"I guess it... felt... right, I guess?"

The spidergirl shook her head in dismay. "You *really* can't be afraid of stepping on my toes in the future, girl."

That statement was just enough to make Sunay suspicious. "And what is *that* supposed to mean, huh?"

Juno grinned broadly, and replied, "Nothin'."

Sunay's eyes narrowed. Juno knew something. "Let me guess, I'm pretty much the only one that doesn't know what this 'surprise' is about."

"Nah. No one's told me nothin," the spidergirl said. "I just know the people involved a good long time. I know the score by now."

"But yer not gonna tell me, are ya?"

"Nope! I wanna see the look on yer face!"

Sunay glowered the rest of the way to the Silver Doubloon, which looked every bit of the wretched dive of a tavern as its name would imply. It was *exactly* the sort of place you'd expect a group of pirates to assemble for a night of cheap drinking.

It was a sore thumb, even in terms of the hovel it resided in: Avalonian in design with weathered gray wood rather than clay, with many of the planks showing signs of neglect, either through rot or coming loose from the frame. The interior didn't strike her as any more impressive. It was well lit, thanks to the torches lining the walls, but that only allowed her to clearly see the poor condition of the bare floorboards and unstained furnishings.

But it was likely the only place that would let the lot of them in while being able to seat *all* of them.

"Ah! There they are!" Ahmin declared jovially from his position directly in front of the bar. He held up his mug with his right hand, and gestured to the table directly before him with his right. "Take a seat, ladies. The night is young, and I think we all got some drinking we want to do!"

A loud cheer followed that statement. "So, does that mean we can finally start?" a question rose from one of the rowing crew in the northeast corner.

Ahmin laughed, a rare sound for the crew to hear. "Yes. It does," he said, taking a long pull from his mug to accentuate the point.

At least the beer wasn't *awful*, thank the Coders for Avalonian brews making it to the First Capital. It was fortunate too, because being suitably buzzed helped Sunay get through what happened next without a total panic.

An hour into the celebration, Jacques stood, barking out to get everyone's attention. “Thank you,” he said once he had received what he sought, the crew going quiet and turning their heads towards the first mate. “I'm sure many of you have figured out that we normally don't have these sort of gatherings, and that something must be up. Well, you're right.”

Even with Jacques's smile, everything else about his expression and body language looked sad. “I hadn't been planning on doing this for a couple of years yet, but... my family is in some tough times. My father recently passed away, and... I'm needed back home.”

Sunay's jaw dropped, reflecting the surprise of the rest of the crew save for the small handful of people at her table. Ahmin stood to clap a comforting hand on Jacques shoulder, and Juno patted his thigh as she held her head down. Bolin and Balco raised their glasses up in respect before setting them back down, their eyes also downcast.

The first mate looked down into his mostly empty glass. “I haven't been home in a *long* time. Coders, my brother and his wife have gone and raised a niece I've never even met. I want to change that. I need to go home. I've done my time and have had my adventures.”

“And where is *that*, before you disappear for the last time?” Juno said in exasperation.

“Oh, nowhere you've ever heard of,” Jacques said, “but I suppose it doesn't do any harm to tell ya all at this point. I come from a little ball of mud called Bakkra. It's literally nothing but a slab of dirt where we farm potatoes and occasionally find precious gems settling in the nearby rivers. Live there for twenty some years, and you'll come to realize why a life on the seas seems appealing.”

He ran his hand through his hair, plucking one gray strand. “But the years are getting' on, and I'm not immortal. Sacili told me that in every muscle in my body for three days after. Add it to everything else... and yeah, it's time. Time to be a responsible, boring old man.”

“Get your rest and peace,” Ahmin said. “You've earned it. At least... starting tomorrow. Tonight, you've still got some partying to do!”

A loud cheer accompanied that statement, followed by an off-key mess of a song that Sunay had overheard the rowing team singing.

*When the storms howl,*
*And bring me down to my knees,*
*All I long for, and desire,*
*Is fair winds and following seas.*

*And in long days,*
*And ages since I've seen trees.*
*All I long for, and desire,*
*Is fair winds and following seas.*

*When the sails end,*
*And it's time to take my last leave,*
*I am glad for, and remember,*
*The fair winds and following seas.*

Jacques tipped an imaginary cap in the direction of the singers, wiping away the beginning of tears in his eyes, then sitting down before he embarrassed himself further, disappearing into his mug and occasionally lifting his head to acknowledge thanks and well wishes from the crew.

It was yet another round before Sunay finally had the guts to speak up, elbowing Juno and teasing, “Well congratulations, you.”

Juno seemed earnestly confused. “For what?”

Sunay pointed lazily towards Jacques, “Well, with the first mate leaving, someone has to take over. Isn't that why you've been teachin' me the rigging?”

Everyone else at the table started chuckling, and Juno's eyebrow raised. “Uh... no. Hasn't Bolin been teaching you how to man the helm?”

Sunay's eyes narrowed to dots. “Oh my... Admiral, you can't possibly be thinkin' of... I mean, I can turn the wheel well enough and all, but Bolin's...”

The chuckles turned into chortles, Bolin having to calm himself between snorts to say, “Goodness no, girl. Balco also was pointin' out tricks o' the trade in the crow's nest, and you were down in the deep with Gurgn, but no one expects you to be a lookout or row!”

Jacques grinned playfully, and said to Ahmin, “You honestly didn't tell her?”

The admiral grinned underneath his mask. “I wanted to see the look on her face. I would have thought learning how to do your job would have been enough of a clue."

Sunay finally put it together. "M... me?"

Ahmin nodded. "We *were* going to wait a couple more years before handing the duties off to someone so young, but Jacques and I think you're ready for the task, and there's no sense keeping him with all the issues back at his home."

"But... there's... Juno... and pits, *everyone* ahead of me in the pecking order!"

"And yet you were the one chosen for the role," Ahmin said. "Had been from the moment you signed on."

"Chosen? By *who*?"

"The Administrators of the Gold Pirates, with my blessing. How they knew... I couldn't say."

Juno poked Sunay back. "*We* all knew it from the get go, but Sacili was no doubt what sold the brass. What told 'em you were ready. You took that mission by the horns there, girl."

"And you're okay with this?" the foxgirl asked.

Jacques snorted. "After a bit of this job, I think you'll discover *exactly* why she's okay with it. The first mate has to be a bit of a jack of all trades. The day to day dealings of the boat is on your head. It's not easy, and it's not always fun."

He and Ahmin locked eyes, and the first mate cracked a smile. "But it's worth it when everything goes right, and you find yourself with the right people."

"I suppose it's presumptuous to assume before I ask," Ahmin said. "So I ask you, do you accept the role as my first mate?"

"Well, I guess I gotta, huh?" the foxgirl said, leaning back in her chair and trying to look confident, even as inside she felt anything but. "Can't disappoint ya now."

~~~~~

It didn't get much better that following morning, and that wasn't the hangover speaking either. Things weren't going to be the same. It was going to be weird not seeing Jacques's stable, constant, reliable presence on the deck. It was even weirder that the crew would now be looking to *her*.

Sunay no longer had a cot, and it certainly wasn't bunked with Juno above her. It wasn't much *better*, she wasn't used to sleeping in a hammock, but she figured she'd get used to it in time. One thing she didn't want to do was disrupt the ship further because she wanted a
~~~~~

freakin' *cot.*

Her cabin wasn't large, maybe ten feet square if she was being generous, but she really had no room to complain considering she had a cabin. She also had a desk with a stack of paper on it, a small chalkboard and chalk that still carried some of Jacques's handwriting at the top where they had been working out the duty rosters together.

The foxgirl decided to leave that handwriting. If it faded with time to become just a memory, so be it, but she wasn't going to be the one to erase it. She couldn't, either literally or figuratively. It wouldn't be right.

Meanwhile, there wasn't much on the docket for today. The crew was still recovering from their night of partying, and even Ahmin was giving them the day to relax and recharge. Shore leave was over, so they had to be on board, but not much else needed doing.

Sunay dressed, again sucking in her breath to get the damn shirt on. One of the things that was coming in today's supply were some new clothes for her, and she hoped that they didn't get bumped for higher priority supplies. Because this was getting ridiculous.

The foxgirl stepped out of her cabin, quietly closing the door behind her. She was on the aft side of the second deck, across from where the upper half of Ahmin's cabin was situated, with a long line of crew cots ahead of her, half of them filled with sleeping crewmates. She didn't want to wake them... not yet. No reason to, after all.

Tiptoeing past, even though she probably could have lit one of Joffe's candles and not roused them, she made it to the stairwell, taking the short rise up to the main deck and the Aramathean morning, bright and colorful from the southern sun and the diamond cliffs.

"Ahoy! First on the deck!"

Sunay barely tilted her head up as Juno dropped down from the aft mast rigging, swinging from a loose rope. "Just playin' with some ideas for the rigging that Joffe scribbled down a while back," she said. "Figure it can't hurt to see if they actually work while we're sittin' here doin' nothin', right?"

"Right," Sunay replied distractedly, moving to the starboard railing, but looking out to sea rather than the cliffs.

Juno followed, putting a friendly arm around the foxgirl's shoulders. "Yer ready for this, ya know that, right?"

Sunay nodded. She wasn't sure how or why she felt that way, but she could honestly say with confidence, "Yeah, I know I am. I jus' need to believe it now."

***To Be Continued...***

**Other works by Thomas Knapp**

The Broken Prophecy

The Sixth Prophet

The Tower of Kartage

For more information, visit http://www.tkocreations.com

**Other works by Fred Gallagher**

MegaTokyo: Volumes 1-3

MegaTokyo Omnibus Vol. 1

*Available from Dark Horse Comics*

MegaTokyo: Volumes 4-6

*Available from DC Comics*

For more information, visit http://www.megatokyo.com or http://www.megagear.com

Made in the USA
San Bernardino, CA
26 March 2016